The
Rebirth
of
Gershon Polokov

The
Rebirth
of
Gershon Polokov

Mindy Littman Holland

SUNSTONE
PRESS

SANTA FE

Sunstone books may be purchased for educational, business, or sales promotional use.
For information please write: Special Markets Department, Sunstone Press,
P.O. Box 2321, Santa Fe, New Mexico 87504-2321.

Book and Cover design ›Vicki Ahl
Body typeface › Lucida Bright
Printed on acid-free paper
∞

Library of Congress Cataloging-in-Publication Data

Holland, Mindy Littman, 1953-
The rebirth of Gershon Polokov / by Mindy Littman Holland.
p. cm.
ISBN 978-0-86534-872-1 (softcovers : alk. paper)
1. Families--Fiction. 2. Reincarnation--Fiction. 3. Domestic fiction. I. Title.
PS3608.O4844R43 2012
813'.6--dc23

2012007598

WWW.SUNSTONEPRESS.COM
SUNSTONE PRESS / POST OFFICE BOX 2321 / SANTA FE, NM 87504-2321 /USA
(505) 988-4418 / ORDERS ONLY (800) 243-5644 / FAX (505) 988-1025

Dedicated to my grandmother,
Ida Schwartz

New York 1956

1

Sophie saw him coming. He was tall with thick dark hair and wide cheekbones. She had seen his face before but couldn't place when or where. She sensed he wasn't coming for bread. The face wore an expression of determination. He had found what he was looking for—three-year-old Sophie. She stopped swirling the tip of her boot in the wood shavings covering the grocery floor and focused on the approaching man.

It was the mid-nineteen fifties in the Bronx and many of the grocery patrons still bore the guttural accents of Eastern Europe. Sophie felt at home there; safe, even when her grandmother's back was turned.

The man came closer. His pale eyes stared straight at her and Sophie stared back. The eyes were tender, almost tearful. Sophie waited for him like a bride at the altar, with a sense of joy and a glimmer of dread.

Nobody else in the store seemed to notice him at all. Sophie had him all to herself. He was a grown man but far younger than her fifty-year-old grandmother and younger than her parents. He knelt from his great height and put a finger to her lips to silence any sound that may come. He didn't know how much the child remembered and didn't want to create a scene. He needed this moment with her.

Sophie looked up anxiously at her grandmother. She didn't want Ida to send him away. She needn't have worried. Ida was concentrating on ordering a seeded rye. Sophie returned her attention to the stranger and smiled. She had been granted a precious moment of privacy.

The man held out his hand. An object shone there, a gold heart, and he gestured for Sophie to take it. Sophie had been taught to not take things from strangers, but this man seemed familiar. Sophie cupped her hand over the heart in the man's palm and felt the cold metal grow warm. She closed her eyes at the vague memory of his touch. Her lips nearly formed his name.

"Put the heart away," came a soft whisper and Sophie obeyed the voice, placing the heart in her coat pocket.

The store became loud with other voices again and Sophie opened her eyes. Ida was snapping her coin purse shut. Sophie frantically searched for the dark-haired man but he had disappeared like a phantom. She felt for the heart in her pocket and, finding it there, she clasped it as if it were his hand. She didn't know where the hand would lead her but she didn't want to let go.

Ida looked down at her and said, "All finished, sweetheart. It's time to go home."

As they left the store, Sophie gave one more look around for the man whose gift she carried. He was gone, but he had left her with a secret. She didn't see him sitting on an orange crate, huddled in his overcoat, watching her leave.

2

Sophie's grandparents lived on the fifth floor of a tenement. The building smelled of cabbage and onions and something earthier, like potatoes left too long in the ground. Sophie trailed her hand along the cool green wall beneath the oak banister that lined the stairwell. Her boots made small slapping sounds against the soiled black-and-white tiles, contrasting with the muted thud of Ida's heels.

Ida sighed each time they reached a landing. She put her shopping bag down on the floor and waited for her heart to stop pounding in her ears before continuing the climb. By the time they reached the third floor, Ida had removed the kerchief from her head and opened the top two buttons of her coat. She looked down at Sophie through thick eyeglasses and said, "Almost there," mostly for her own reassurance. Sophie leaned against her grandmother's Clorox-scented hand. The small face was flushed.

Ida bent over to open Sophie's quilted overcoat and Sophie quickly pushed a hand in her pocket, wrapping her fingers around the heart.

"What's the matter, are you still cold?" Ida asked.

Sophie said, "No."

Ida removed the child's woolen hat and patted her damp hair. "Do you want to ride the rest of the way?" she asked.

Sophie shook her head.

Relieved, Ida straightened up, pressing a fist into the small of her back. The climb to the apartment was getting more difficult for her, but there was no choice but to continue. When they finally arrived, Ida vowed for the hundredth time that year that they would move to an apartment with an elevator.

A warm blast of steam heat and a hint of boiled chicken greeted them as they walked into the cramped foyer. Ida clicked the light switch, turning on a sconce. The grayed wallpaper absorbed most of the light, leaving the hallway in perpetual dusk.

"Let's get these heavy coats off," said Ida.

She slowly sank to the floor on her arthritic knees and smiled at Sophie. The child held out her arms and studied Ida's face. When her hands were free, she used them to smooth Ida's wrinkles.

"You like Grandma's pleats?" Ida asked.

She playfully bit at one of Sophie's outstretched fingers. Sophie quickly pulled her hand back. They had played this game before.

"Do it again, Gram," she said.

"We'll play more later. It's time to wash up and cook. Grandpa will be home soon."

Ida turned Sophie's coat upside down to swat off a bit of sawdust and the gold heart clattered to the hardwood floor. Sophie dropped to her knees to retrieve it, but Ida moved with unusual speed and swept it up.

"What's this?" she asked, peering at the heart beneath her glasses in the dim light.

Sophie looked at her feet and said, "It's a charm."

"Where did it come from?" asked Ida, rubbing the intricate engraving.

Sophie fidgeted. "It's mine."

It wasn't a lie. Somebody had given it to her and now it was hers. Ida didn't need to know the whole truth.

Ida opened the heart and pursed her lips when she saw what lay within. On the right, was a picture of her mother; on the left, was her father. They were already old and their expressions were blank as they stared out from their tiny frames.

3

Ida asked, "Did you know there were pictures in this locket, Sophie?"

Sophie shook her head. Ida held the heart open for her to see and the child's eyes welled with tears. Memories she didn't understand rattled her.

"Why are you crying? Do you recognize these people?"

Sophie nodded and stared at Ida. She wondered when Ida had gotten so old.

Ida asked, "Who are they?"

Sophie's voice was barely audible when she said, "Daddy and me."

Ida didn't know what to say. The man in the picture looked nothing like Sophie's father. She wondered if Sophie was overtired from the walk up the infernal stairs and placed a hand on her granddaughter's forehead. It was cool to the touch. She asked, "Do you want to lie down for a while?"

Sophie shook her head.

Ida said, "You know the man in the picture is *my* father, not yours."

Sophie looked solemn and said, "I know that. That's what I said."

Ida shook her head and wondered why her granddaughter was so confused. Sophie had had only the briefest of meetings with her great-grandfather before he died and she hadn't known her great-grandmother, Sofia, at all. Sofia had died a year before Sophie was born. When Sophie came around, she was given Sofia's name. Ida had been particularly pleased that her mother was honored in this way and felt an instant kinship with the baby. Her first words to Sophie were, "*You* are my mommy now."

Sophie had looked back at her grandmother with ancient eyes

that raised chills on Ida's arms. Ida had called out, "She's looking at me as if she knows me." What Ida couldn't know was what Sophie saw the first time she set eyes on her grandmother. The infant had looked backward and forward into the eyes of her own daughter.

The vision had quickly passed. In the three years since her birth, Sophie had only seen Ida as her grandmother, but Ida had never forgotten the feeling of reconnection with her own mother. Sophie was no ordinary child.

Ida looked at the picture of her father. Was it possible that Sophie remembered him? He had died the night Sophie was brought home from the hospital. It had been an odd night. The old man had spent his last hour with Sophie and didn't want to let her go. Ida wondered what had gone on behind closed doors in the moments before Sophie was removed from his reluctant arms and taken home. What had he told her?

While Ida ruminated, Sophie patted her hand and said, "Close the heart, Gram. We had secrets. I'll tell you about them someday."

Ida stared at her granddaughter's guileless face and asked, "What secrets?"

Sophie said, "Today is not the day for secrets." She took the locket from her grandmother and clicked it firmly shut.

4

When Sophie opened her eyes the next morning, she was lying in her grandmother's arms in her grandparents' big bed. Morning light seeped feebly in beneath the drawn window shade. Sophie was in no hurry to rise. She snuggled more deeply into her grandmother's embrace and listened to Ida's whistling breath. Sophie knew she would be going home with her parents and brother that day. They felt like strangers to her. She didn't want to leave the warm familiarity of her grandparents' apartment.

Sophie stiffened when she heard a gentle knocking at the bedroom door. Ida's eyes fluttered open and squinted at the bedside clock. "Let's go back to sleep for a few hours," she said, holding Sophie tighter.

The knocking continued. Sophie turned her head and saw her grandfather, Gabe, peeking at them from the door. He was fully dressed in a long-sleeved, buttoned-down white shirt and expertly ironed pants, but no tie. It was Saturday. He wouldn't be going to the tailor shop that day.

Gabe asked, "Is everybody awake?"

"No, we're sleeping," mumbled Ida.

"It's almost nine o'clock," said Gabe. "They'll be here soon."

Sophie shuddered. Why did she need to leave the safety and calmness of this place, the soothing routines and familiar aromas? The only time she enjoyed being home was when she was spending time with her friend, Lila. Lila lived downstairs and was very old, older than Sophie's grandparents. Sophie stayed with Lila when her mother wanted to be alone or was busy with her card-party ladies. Lila made her feel like a grown-up.

Ida moved her gaze down to the little girl nestled against her, a small, warm presence. "Time to get up, sweetheart," she said. Neither stirred.

Gabe had left his post by the door and returned a few minutes later with two glasses of orange juice.

Ida propped herself up on a pillow before accepting a kiss and a glass. Gabe helped Sophie hold the heavy tumbler, guiding it toward her mouth. "It's flurrying out," he said.

"It sure isn't snowing in here," said Ida, fanning her flushed face. "I'm roasting." Ida tossed off the flowered quilt and pulled her thin flannel nightgown back from her body. She blew down between her heavy breasts.

Gabe went to the window and raised the blind. He pounded the glass once with the heels of his hands and slid the window up enough to chill the air. "Smells like snow, all right," he said.

As he stood in the bright white light, inhaling deeply, Sophie began to scream. Gabe choked out a cold breath as he ran to her side. "Sophie, what is it?" he asked.

Sophie pointed a thin finger at the empty rocker in front of the window and quavered, "It's the old man."

"What old man?" asked Gabe. "I'm the only old man here and I'm not sitting down."

"Not you, Papa. The man from the picture is sitting in the chair."

"What picture?" asked Gabe. "What's she talking about, Ida?"

Gabe walked to the chair and wiped his hand across the seat. Sophie had buried her head under Ida's arm and in a muffled voice said, "Make him go away. I'm not ready."

Gabe said, "Sophie, there's nobody in the chair. "Open your eyes and look."

Keeping her face hidden, Sophie said, "Close the blinds, Papa."

Gabe looked at Ida and gestured his confusion with open hands. Ida said, "It's okay, Gabe. Let's send the old man away." Gabe closed the blinds and Sophie's tense body relaxed.

"What's this about a picture?" Gabe asked, returning to the side of the bed.

"Do you want to show Grandpa what you had in your pocket, Sophie?"

Feeling betrayed, Sophie raised her head and said, "That was a secret."

"What's all this about?" asked Gabe.

Ida raised her eyebrow at Sophie and said, "Grandpa can keep a secret."

Sophie wasn't prone to dramatics and Ida didn't expect much of a battle now. Theirs was a relationship of unspoken trust.

Sophie looked at her grandfather, a good man, and reluctantly said, "Okay."

Ida kissed her cheek and said, "Sophie has a locket with pictures of my parents in it. You probably took them yourself. She just saw them for the first time yesterday and, for some reason, the pictures scared her."

Gabe sat at the edge of the bed and cupped his granddaughter's chin.

"There's nothing to fear, Sophie. Your great-grandfather loved you very much and your great-grandmother would've been crazy about you. They would never harm you. Do you understand?"

Sophie nodded at her grandfather but her eyes remained focused on the window. The chair may have looked empty but Sophie knew whom she saw. It was the man from the store, the bearer of the heart, the love of her life, the man she would grow old with. The stranger had a name now and it was the same as her great-grandfather's name. His name was Gershon Polokov, but the memory was gone before Sophie could speak it.

5

Sophie observed her family from behind her grandmother's legs. They smelled of overheated Persian lamb, cashmere and leather and their boots oozed water.

"That's quite a climb," said Sophie's father, Bill, as he kissed Ida's cheek and shook Gabe's extended hand.

Sophie's six-year-old brother, Ron, wrapped his arms around his grandmother's thighs, looking up. Ida bent at the waist and covered his face in kisses, wiping away lipstick smudges with her thumbs. When Ida released him, he turned his attention to his grandfather who picked him up with a groan and said, "Look at how big he's getting."

Sophie continued to hide her face in the folds of her grandmother's dress.

"Where's Sophie?" asked Sophie's mother, Roma. "Do you think she'll remember me?"

Sophie, look who's here," said Ida. "Do you know who that is?"

Sophie peaked out from behind Ida's hip and gazed up at her mother's face. She recognized the full lips, painted blood red, the watery blue eyes and the slightly askew nose.

"Mommy," she said quietly.

Roma said, "Bill, pick her up for me, will you? I shouldn't be bending or lifting yet."

Sophie knew her mother had spent the past couple of weeks at the hospital. Roma had had an adhesions operation, but Ida told Sophie her mother had had a bellyache.

Sophie's father swept her up in his arms and kissed her cheek. His chin, already bristly after an early-morning shave, chafed her China-doll skin. Bill brought her over to Roma.

Roma took Sophie's face in her hands and kissed her hard on both cheeks, leaving florid lipstick stains and an after-scent of cigarettes.

"Did you miss Mother Dear?" she asked.

Her smile was tarnished with nicotine.

Sophie didn't respond fast enough. She was busy studying her mother's face. By the time she said, "Yes," Roma's red lips had already turned down.

"I need a smoke," she said.

She turned her back and headed for the kitchen.

After a few seconds of awkward shuffling, Gabe said, "So, take off your coats and stay a while. You must be starved."

6

B ill carried a sleeping Sophie up the long flight of stairs to their garden apartment in Flushing, followed by his exhausted wife and dawdling son. Someday, they would have to find a place on the ground floor.

He opened the door into the living room and brought Sophie into her bedroom, a small space beside the kitchen. Sophie barely stirred as he removed her outer clothes and deposited her, belly-up, on her bed. Ida had dressed her in a flannel nightgown before they'd left for home, so all Bill had to do was pull up the yellow blanket and shut the light.

For once, Ron went directly to his room without argument. He was told that if he was very good, his grandparents would move to Queens and he would get to see them more often. Bill went to help Ron get into his Roy Rogers pajamas, oversee the tooth-brushing process and sing a few verses of *I Met An Old Lady Who Swallowed a Fly* before kissing the boy good night.

Roma hung her coat and sank into the sapphire-and-gold brocade couch in the living room. She removed her shoes with a sigh and took a Newport out of a silver box on the Danish modern coffee table. Lighting the cigarette, she inhaled deeply, waving the match to extinguish the flame. Roma closed her eyes and thought about what being home meant.

While she was in the hospital, their downstairs neighbors, Jeanette, and her elderly mother, Lila, had taken care of Ron after school, until Bill got home from work. Most nights, Jeanette fed them both.

Now, Roma would be in charge of the children and the meals, the milk spills, the muddy boots and the sticky hands, the relentless cheerfulness of it, the utter boredom. Then, she would need to see to

Bill's needs at night. She puffed on her cigarette, a deep furrow between her brows, feeling home pushing down on her shoulders.

On Monday, Roma could get back into her card game. She was having the girls over for five-handed poker. She would fix a tuna salad and defrost a Sara Lee pound cake. Bill would be at work, Ron at school and Sophie downstairs with Lila.

Always a big winner, Roma got excited at the prospect of raking the ladies over the coals in their nickel and dime game. The wad of bills in her cardboard jewelry box was getting fatter, the coin collection heavier. Roma's palms itched in anticipation of getting back into action.

Bill came into the living room, freshly-shaven and wearing a clean, white undershirt. He was a handsome, broad-shouldered man with curly black hair on the verge of thinning. He began to cough. Roma was pulled back to Saturday night with the prospect of Sunday looming and she sunk into the couch.

"You're going to kill me with those things," Bill half-joked, swatting at the smoky air. Roma gave him a look and said, "Leave me alone, already, with the cigarettes."

Bill sighed and sat beside Roma, putting his arm around her shoulder. Roma stiffened slightly, then relented. He didn't deserve her anger, but he was always so damned accommodating.

"How do you feel, honey?" Bill asked. "Can I get you anything?"

"I just want to sit here a minute. I've got a splitting headache."

Roma rubbed the crease between her brows.

Bill said, "Why don't you go make yourself comfortable? I'll help you."

Roma said, "Can I just sit here in peace for a minute? I must've climbed a hundred steps today." She turned away from him and took a deep drag, letting the smoke fill her mouth.

"The kids are asleep, at least," Bill said, still cheerful, still hopeful.

Stretching his long legs in front of him, Bill lifted his arms over his head and yawned like a lion. He said, "It's been a tiring day. I think I'll watch a little news and call it a night."

He got up to turn on the Magnavox in the blond console. Roma crushed her cigarette out and rose, hissing between her teeth. She pinched her boots between two fingers and headed for the bedroom without a word.

Bill watched her back disappear into the hallway. He put his hands behind his head and stared at the ceiling, a toothpick wiggling between his lips. Roma had been away for two weeks. When she was around, Bill often wondered what he had done wrong.

7

Sometime in the night, Sophie woke up disoriented and alone. She was home, no longer surrounded by her grandmother's moist, warm arms. As her eyes adjusted to the dark, Sophie saw the outline of a man hovering over her. A scream started in the back of her throat and froze. She recognized him. She knew he'd come back.

The man took Sophie's face in his hands and whispered, "Remember me?" Sophie nodded into his palm and tasted wintergreen.

"Are you afraid?" he asked.

"No," she said. "What's taken you so long to find me?"

The man lowered his head and put his face directly in front of Sophie's. She had always loved his broad face. The irises of his eyes were nearly clear in the dim room and they seemed to emit their own light.

"I never lost you," he said.

He kissed her lightly on the lips and took Sophie into his arms. Against his chest, Sophie was lulled back to sleep by the slow rhythm of his heart.

Sophie was awake when Bill came to look in on her the next morning. A bright sun blasted through the blinds and filled the room with striped light.

"Good morning, chicken. It was so quiet in here, I'm surprised to see you awake."

"Where did Gershon go?" asked Sophie.

Bill sat down at the foot of her narrow bed and asked, "Gershon who, honey?"

"The man."

"I don't know who you're talking about," said Bill, looking around the small room. "You just had a dream, honey. There's no man here."

"Can I dream with my eyes open?"

Bill bent down and took his daughter by her shoulders. Looking her in the eyes, he said, "There was no man here, Sophie. You had a dream."

"There *was* a man here," Sophie insisted. "He came for me."

"Really," said Bill. "Well, who was he?"

"Gershon."

"The only Gershon I ever knew was your great-grandfather and he hasn't been around since you were born. Was your visitor an old man?"

Sophie shook her head.

"Was he a young man?"

"Yes."

Growing more concerned, Bill asked, "Did he touch you?"

"Yes," said Sophie. "He touched me here," she said, putting a hand to her jaw. "He kissed me here," she said, touching her lips. "Then, he hugged me and I fell asleep."

Bill visually inspected his daughter and asked, "Did you ever see this man at Grandma and Grandpa's house?"

Sophie nodded, but she didn't want to tell her father about the man in the store or the gold heart or the old man by the window. Now that she was back in her bedroom in Flushing, she felt very confused. She said, "I saw pictures and had memories."

Bill wondered what kind of memories his young daughter could possibly have. He asked, "Did you recognize the man?"

Sophie stroked her thin arms and said, "He was someone who loved me."

Bill took a hard look at his daughter and said, "I'd like to see this young man who comes in the night. If he comes again, you must yell for me, understand?"

Sophie nodded.

"Where's Mommy?" she asked, anxious to change the subject.

"Still asleep."

"Wake her up," she said.

Bill obediently went off to oblige his daughter. He entered his darkened bedroom and saw his wife buried up to her neck in quilts with a look of profound abandon on her face. He wondered what she was dreaming about. Maybe an amorous young man was visiting her in the night, too.

The rickety brass headboard rattled and the mattress crunched beneath Bill's hip as he sat on the edge of the bed and placed his hand lightly on Roma's blanketed shoulder. "Honey, it's late," said Bill, quietly. "Are you going to get up today?"

Roma's eyes fluttered. "Go away, I'm sleeping," she mumbled into her pillow.

"Sophie is asking for you."

"What time is it?" Roma asked.

"Nearly nine. Time to get up. Are you feeling okay? You were asleep when I got in last night. I didn't want to wake you."

Bill sat and fidgeted in the uncomfortable silence. He became aware of Sophie's tiny silhouette at the door. Her presence brightened his tone.

"Come in, Sophie," he said. "Did you want to say 'good morning' to Mother?"

Roma cleared her throat and said, "How's my precious girl? Come up into the bed with me."

Sophie went to the side of the bed. Roma dragged her onto the mattress and entrapped her in her arms. Pulling her close, Roma drifted off into the apple-scented memory of pomade in Sophie's hair. She wanted to sleep until Monday, but it was still the damned weekend and she had a husband and kids to deal with.

8

Sophie sat opposite Lila at the kitchen table drawing the old woman's portrait with crayons. Lila had long gray hair that hung down the back of her handmade knit sweater like dirty rags and dark rings beneath her filmy eyes. She wore a flowery housedress with heavy black shoes and support hose.

Lila never left the apartment, not even to pick up the newspaper. Her skin was as withered and pale as pressed camellia blossoms and splotched with age spots. Sophie was a sensitive artist, capturing more than mere features.

"Are you going to die soon?" asked Sophie.

Lila smiled, displaying a row of perfect dentures, and said, "Yes, I'm going to die soon."

"Where are you going to go when you die?"

"I don't know, darling. Heaven, I hope."

Sophie applied crayon to paper, coloring in the flowers on Lila's muumuu.

"Is Gram going to die, too?"

"Yes, darling. Everything that lives dies someday. But, your grandmother is young. She won't die for a long, long time. She's young enough to be my daughter."

"You are very old," said Sophie.

"Yes, I'm the same age as your Nana Sofia would've been. Did you know, Sophie, that I knew your great-grandmother in the Old Country? We lived in the same house and came over on the same boat. She would've adored you."

Sophie kept drawing, allowing the old woman a moment of reminiscence.

"When we came to America, your great-grandfather introduced me to a nice man. We married and had Jeanette. Your Grandma Ida used to look after her. Ida and Jeanette became close friends. So you see, little Sophie, we are all like one family."

Sophie looked up from her drawing and asked, "Am I going to die?"

Lila studied Sophie's face, rapt in concentration over her drawing and said, "Not for a long, long, *long* time. What's all this talk about dying? You're a beautiful little girl with your whole life ahead of you. You mustn't worry about dying."

"Will Gershon come for me when I die?"

"Who's Gershon?"

"My husband."

Lila chuckled and said, "Goodness, Sophie. You're only three years old."

"I'm twenty-two."

Lila threw up her hands and laughed, "What an imagination. Wait until your mother hears this. You are such a funny child."

Sophie lifted her crayon from the paper and looked into Lila's eyes. "Why are you laughing?" she asked, her small features hardening.

Lila's mirth disappeared.

"I'm sorry, Sophie. I never received a wedding invitation. How was I supposed to know you got married?"

"You were the only one there," said Sophie.

Lila broke out in a sweat. She tugged at the neck of her sweater and said, "I guess I don't remember, Sophie. Can you draw me a picture of your husband?"

Sophie nodded and turned the portrait of Lila over. She selected a black crayon and started to draw. A face emerged, with wide cheekbones and a long, angular nose. The mouth was drawn closed, in a curved line. The colorless eyes stared under fine brows. Black hair spiraled to his shoulders. Lila stared at the picture and clearly recognized the face that Sophie drew. She thought about the first time she'd seen it.

Lila had worked as a nursemaid for the Chayevsky's, a wealthy family in Moscow. One day, a six-year-old named Sofia was brought in from Odessa to help with the cooking. Sofia's mother had died in childbirth. Her father was a religious man who quickly remarried. His new wife refused to take care of his young children. Sofia was sent to live with the Chayevsky's as an indentured servant. She was expected to do a grownup's work, but was little more than a baby. Lila took care of her, taught her the rules of the house and eventually became her friend.

Sofia was still living with the Chayevsky's when she met a young man on the way home from the market. Sofia was twenty-one and already considered an old maid. Gershon Polokov was a seventeen-year old tailor's apprentice. As young as he was, he was ready for a wife and Sofia was an alluring older woman, eager for love. They agreed to marry and asked Lila to be their witness.

The newlyweds found a small apartment on the rough outskirts of the city. Sofia and Lila fell out of touch and Sofia found herself living amid unfriendly strangers. It was the early nineteen hundreds and Russia was engaged in war with the Japanese.

One day, on his way home from work, Gershon was kidnapped by soldiers and conscripted into the Tsar's army. Sofia was already expecting their first child. Proud and practical, she set out to find work. She sewed buttons on army uniforms for pennies. The meager pay did not keep her from losing her apartment and starving. Her face grew thin and the fluttery kicks inside of her slowed and ceased.

Sofia gave birth to a full-term stillborn son in the charity ward of the city hospital. The infant was wrapped in newspaper and disposed of before Sofia could see his face. The hospital released her back to the streets; sick, weak and penniless. Giving up hope of ever seeing her husband again, Sofia made her way back to the Chayevsky's. Lila nursed her back to health.

Six months later, Gershon escaped from the army. He was on his way to the Far East when his train stopped in the middle of nowhere. He jumped from the train and ran. He hid in a haystack in a farmer's barn. Soldiers sent to retrieve him ransacked the farm and stabbed the haystack with bayonets. Miraculously, he avoided their thrusts and detection. When they gave up their search, Gershon began the perilous journey back home to Moscow on foot.

Moving furtively from shadow to shadow, Gershon went to the small apartment he had shared with Sofia. The landlord told him Sofia was long gone and that she hadn't left a forwarding address. He told Gershon that he threw Sofia out when she couldn't pay the rent. Gershon lunged at the man and wrapped one gigantic hand around his throat until the landlord gasped, "I couldn't help it. I needed the money." Gershon released the man and staggered away.

On that same moonless night, he made his way to the Chayevsky's. Lila gasped when she opened the kitchen door and saw his gaunt, heavily bearded face. She hissed, "Where have you been? We thought you were dead."

"I've been keeping company with the Tsar," he said. "I jumped off a train on the way to the front lines. If they catch me, I will be dead. Tell, me, Lila, do you know where Sofia is?"

"Sofia is here. Quick, come inside before somebody sees you," she said, tugging on his coat sleeve. "Let me go get her."

Gershon ran a hand through his long, tangled hair as he waited for his wife to appear. Sofia barely stopped to look at him as she fell into his arms. They held each other for a long time, first in silence, then in frantic whispers, then with quiet tears. When they finally looked at each other, they stared as if seeing a ghost.

Lila touched Sofia lightly on the arm and said, "Go to my room and lock the door. We'll figure out what you must do later."

"Can I stay here?" Gershon asked.

"Where else are you to go?" said Lila. "Of course, you must stay here, but hidden, Gershon. The Chayevsky's will be away in St. Petersburg another week. When they return, you will have to make other arrangements. They took Sofia in when she needed help. We mustn't place them at risk."

Gershon's eyes never left Sofia. "I must leave Russia as soon as possible."

"No," said Sofia, groping his arms. "You just came back to me. I can't lose you again."

"Shhhh," he said, putting a finger to her lips. "I am a deserter. It will be too dangerous for you to travel with me. You must stay here. I will go to America. When I get settled, I will send for you. I will send for Lila, too, if she wants to come. Russia is not safe for any of us anymore."

"With what will you get there?" asked Sofia.

"My uncle will send me the money for a steamboat ticket," said Gershon. "He has a tailor shop in New York. I will go to work there. I should be able to send for you within a year."

Gershon stayed with Sofia for a week before traveling to Estonia, where he was issued a visa at the American Consulate. When permission was granted to immigrate to the United States, he began a long journey that brought him to Southhampton, England. He was detained in Atlantic Park until immigration quotas were satisfied and then he sailed to New York on the SS Olympic, just another dark, bearded face in steerage.

The year was nineteen oh six. Gershon went to work for his uncle in the lower east side of New York. By the time he was able to send for Sofia and Lila, Sofia had given birth to a healthy baby girl, named Itka. In America, the little girl would be known as Ida, Sophie's grandmother.

9

Seventy-three-year-old Lila sat in her kitchen in Flushing staring at a drawing of a face she hadn't seen in a half a century. She watched as little Sophie filled in the details of her great-grandfather's face. The young Gershon emerged from the paper. Lila shuddered once as his clear eyes connected with hers and brought her beguilingly into his light. She slumped against the table, her head falling to her chest.

The late afternoon sun angled across Sophie's face. She climbed down from her chair and kissed Lila's limp, cool hand. She knew that Lila was dead. There was no need to go tearing up the stairs. A strand of Lila's hair draped over the side of the table. Sophie held it against her cheek and cried, "Oh, Lila, I will miss you for a long time. The next time we meet, you won't know me. But, I will know you."

When the sun had lowered and the kitchen had gone gray, Sophie turned the picture of Gershon over and left Lila's portrait face-up on the table before leaving the apartment. Reaching up for the banister, Sophie walked slowly upstairs to her own apartment and knocked on the door. She heard laughing women inside. She stood there waiting to be heard. The raucous hilarity continued until Sophie pounded on the door with her fists. The noise inside abruptly ceased and she heard the sound of feet approaching. Her mother opened the door.

"What's wrong?" asked Roma, looming over her. A scent of smoke and hairspray filled the stairwell and made Sophie's eyes water.

"Lila's dead," announced Sophie.

Upon hearing the news, Jeanette's chair tipped over and sent her sprawling backwards onto the living room floor, setting off shrieks of alarm from the other women. Jeanette was lying on her back like a fallen roach, her short legs flailing in the air. The women grabbed Jeanette by the arms and hauled her up. They flew down the stairs like a flock of terrified birds.

Roma pulled Sophie into the apartment and said, "You stay here. Go lay down on my bed. Don't touch anything. I'll be up soon."

Sophie lay on her parents' bed and listened to the chorus of screams from below. She was glad that Lila couldn't hear them.

10

Ida went to Jeanette's apartment after Lila's funeral to start rolling cold cuts and slicing rolls in half. The others would be down shortly. When the two women entered the kitchen, Ida saw a drawing taped to the side of the refrigerator.

"Jeanette," she said, "who drew this?"

"My mother was babysitting for Sophie on the day she died. I found the drawing on the table beside her. I assume Sophie drew it. It's an awfully good drawing for a little girl, isn't it?"

Ida lowered her glasses as she took a closer look. "Yes, it's amazingly good. Are you sure Sophie drew it?"

"Who else?" Jeanette asked. "Mama couldn't draw. Why do you ask?"

"Because I'm wondering how my little Sophie could have known what your mother looked like as a girl."

"What are you talking about?" said Jeanette, raising her own glasses. "That's *me*, not Mama. It doesn't look exactly like me, but what do you expect from a three-year-old?"

"I don't expect her to know what your mother looked like as a very young woman, unless you have a picture laying around here somewhere."

"I don't have any pictures of my mother as a girl."

"Well, you do now, Jeanette. That's your mother, I'm telling you. Look at the eyes."

Jeanette removed the picture from the refrigerator to take a closer look and shivered. "I don't understand it," she said, shaking her head.

When Ida spotted the picture on the back, she said, "And, that's my father as a young man."

"No," said Jeanette.

She gazed at the striking features and said, "Oh, Ida."

"I remember when he looked like that," said Ida. "He was still just a boy when I was born."

Jeanette looked sideways at Ida and said, "Well, this is just incredible. Maybe my mother was a better artist than I thought. Maybe she had a sudden burst of creativity before she died. Maybe she was trying to tell us something."

"Maybe," said Ida, not wanting to upset her friend. "She certainly knew my father as a young man."

"I wouldn't be here without your father."

"That makes the two of us," said Ida, hugging Jeanette. "Keep these drawings. They were a gift to you."

Jeanette taped the drawings back on the refrigerator door and patted them lovingly in place.

"I know your parents had their difficulties, but I miss your father," she said. "He was always so comforting to be around."

"He couldn't go on after my mother died," said Ida. "But, he did live long enough to see his two great-grandchildren. He loved them both, but he was particularly enthralled with Sophie. I'm so glad he got to spend a little time with her."

"I think he saw a little Sofia in her," said Jeanette.

"Yes," said Ida. "I see it, too."

The doorbell rang and Jeanette went into the living room to open the door. Roma and Bill were there with Gabe, Ron and Sophie. Both children wrapped their arms around Jeanette's hips and Gabe kissed her on the cheek.

"How you doing, honey?" he asked. "What can I do for you?"

"Would you mind covering the mirrors for me, Gabe? I have a couple of big towels on the bed."

"Sure, sweetheart. Right away." Gabe headed into Jeanette's bedroom.

Roma and Bill sat on Jeanette's chintz-covered couch, each with a child standing between their knees.

"Sit down," said Roma to Jeanette. "You must be exhausted and you'll have a crowd here soon."

"I'm not expecting such a crowd," said Jeanette, still standing. "We have very little family left."

Jeanette and her deceased husband never had any children.

"You've got to see what Mama drew before she died."

Jeanette ran into the kitchen and brought back Lila's portrait. She held it up for all to see.

"Sophie, do you recognize this drawing?" Jeanette asked.

Sophie nodded.

"Who is this?" Jeanette asked.

"It's Lila." Sophie looked up at Jeanette through long eyelashes.

"Who drew it?" Jeanette asked.

"I did," said Sophie. "Lila was my best friend."

Jeanette handed the picture to Roma and asked, "What do you make of this?"

Roma took the picture from Jeanette and shivered.

"It resembles your mother, but this is a picture of a girl, not an old woman." Roma handed the picture to Ida and said, "Ma, what do you think?"

"That's a young Lila," said Ida. "Come here, little one," she said to Sophie, extending both arms.

Sophie freed herself from her mother's legs and Ida lifted her, hugging her tightly to her chest.

"You knew Lila very well, didn't you?" she whispered in the child's ear.

Ida felt the nod against her chin and said, "How wonderful, how wonderful."

"What's going on?" asked Bill.

"Sophie is a very special girl," said Ida.

She visualized her mother's face, small and round, with intelligent eyes and slightly sardonic smile. She struggled to contain her excitement. This would be her and Sophie's secret. The others couldn't begin to understand. The question was why had she come back. What did she want?

"What do you want, little Sophie?" she asked.

"*Borscht*," said Sophie.

Ida almost clapped.

"Will somebody please tell me what's going on here?" exploded Bill, from the couch. "Why is my three-year-old asking for *borscht*? And what's the deal with the drawings?"

Ida just laughed and said, "Sophie is a true Polokov. Maybe she craves a taste of the mother country. So, she likes beets. At least she didn't ask for *ptcha*. As for the drawings, I have no explanation. They are just children's drawings. Perhaps they resemble Lila and Gershon in their earlier days, but so what? Let's not make too much of it."

"*Ptcha*, for Christ's sake!" ranted Bill. "Who in their right mind would ask for jellied calves feet? I don't like this. A few days ago, she was talking about seeing a man in her room. I don't understand what's going on with her."

Roma lowered her cigarette lighter and asked, "What man? You didn't say anything to me about a man."

"She called him Gershon, same as your grandfather's name," said Bill. "She told me that he touched her face and kissed her. What kind of a fantasy is that for a three-year-old to have?"

Sophie looked at her father with a blank expression. She didn't know what he was talking about, nor did she recognize the face of the man in the picture. She was a three-year-old girl being held by her grandmother in a familiar room, surrounded by family. Her mother was home from the hospital. Her father fixed her Cheerios in the morning. Her brother gave her sips of his chocolate milk. Sophie had never tasted beet soup.

"I'm sleepy," she said, putting her head down on Ida's shoulder.

"She's had a rough few days," said Ida. "She needs to lie down. Where should I put her, Jeanette?"

"Why don't you put her on my mother's bed?"

Ida carried the nodding child away and placed her on the afghan coverlet. She arranged a row of pillows against the bed's brass rails and covered Sophie with a shawl she found folded neatly on a straight-backed chair. Sophie slept so soundlessly Ida placed the back of her hand in front of her nose to make sure she was breathing. She felt like keeping watch over her granddaughter, protecting her from uninvited company, but she knew her presence was required elsewhere.

"You're safe, mommy," she whispered. "I'll be right outside your door."

She drew the curtains and left the room, leaving the door partly ajar.

While she slept sandwiched between the afghan and the shawl, Sophie inhaled Lila's homey scent. Visions of Lila's smiling face wisped just behind Sophie's eyelids. Sophie licked her lips and tasted teaberry. Turning on her side, she twitched as she felt a man's weight, both heavy and light, suddenly pressed against her back. He draped an arm around her stomach and pulled her against him. The arm was bare and corded with muscle. She couldn't open her eyes.

"Don't be afraid," the man whispered.

Sophie relaxed into the man's embrace.

"Good," he said. "You know my voice. You will hear it from time to time, but you will not see my face again until you are grown and ready to receive me. I will never harm you, but I am not entirely benign. We are spirits reborn, and we are destined to be together. Someday, when you're grown, our paths will cross and our lives will join. Your grandmother already senses our union, but she won't betray us. You are a part of me and I will take you back. For now, you must be an unencumbered child."

The man bowed his head against the back of Sophie's shoulder and pulled her close, gently pressing a cool hand against her upper abdomen. The pressure abruptly ceased.

Fully awake now, Sophie tossed the shawl aside as the heat between her legs made its way up the middle of her chest. She crept down from the day bed and walked into the living room rubbing her eyes.

The seed had been planted.

Massachusetts 1974

11

Sophie lived with three other women and their temporary boyfriends in a ramshackle rental house with cobalt blue shutters and a weed-choked vegetable garden on Oak Street in Brighton, Massachusetts. They were all Boston University seniors, preparing to graduate in the spring of nineteen seventy-five.

Sophie was dating a long-limbed political science major named Bob, who looked at her with love-struck eyes and asked permission to kiss her. She would've preferred it if he had just kissed her.

It was in the month of Bob that the call came from Ida. It was December. Sophie and Bob were lying in bed with their legs entwined when the phone rang. They were staring at the ceiling in afterglow, blowing smoke rings. Sophie's tabby was on top of the headboard, languidly swatting at the diaphanous puffs. Sophie's bulimic housemate stopped puking long enough to knock on Sophie's door and say, "Phone for you."

Sophie swung her long, slender legs over the side of the bed and rose, stretching upward on her toes. Bob looked at Sophie's muscular back, admiring the pronounced curve of her waist. "I'll be right back," she said, settling back down to earth and pulling on Bob's threadbare flannel shirt that had been dangling from a bedpost. It came down to the middle of her thighs.

Sophie shivered as she walked into the cold kitchen. One of the house boyfriends was fixing a cup of coffee and wiggling his narrow hips to the reggae beat of *The Harder They Come*.

"Can you turn it down a little?" asked Sophie. She gestured at the phone. The young man eyeballed her bare legs and took his time moseying over to the radio to lower the volume.

Sophie said, "Thank you, Bob Marley," and turned her back for privacy. "Hello," she said into the receiver.

"Sophie?"

Sophie stiffened when she heard her grandmother's voice made reedy by some unknown malady. Sophie's throat tightened. Her grandmother never called her, certainly not over long distance. Sophie fought to keep her own voice calm. She set to work tugging on her long, wild mop of hair.

"Gram?" she said.

"Sophie, I need to go in for an operation."

Sophie placed a hand against the wall to steady herself. With her eyes closed, she visualized her robust Grandma Ida dancing into her girdle singing *Twist and Shout.*

"Sophie? Are you there?"

Sophie opened her eyes and asked, "What kind of operation?"

"Gallbladder."

Lyndon Johnson came to mind, lifting his shirt to show off his surgery scar. Sophie didn't want to think about a scalpel cutting into her grandmother's soft white flesh. She wondered why her grandmother sounded like a cricket. Ida's voice was too high by a complete octave.

"When and where is the surgery?"

"Tomorrow morning, at the Long Island Jewish Hospital."

"I'm coming home," said Sophie.

"There's no need to rush home. I just wanted to hear your voice before the operation. It's just my gallbladder, no cause for alarm. I don't want you to worry."

Ida sounded reassuring, but the voice was too thin, too wire-fine. Sophie tried to pummel the kernel of fright in her chest with practicality. Surely, Gram could live very nicely without a gallbladder.

"I'm coming home," said Sophie again, and Ida didn't argue.

Sophie replaced the receiver and walked slowly back into her room. Bob was lying on his back, an arm thrown behind his head. Sophie sat on the bed and broke into tears.

"My God, who was that?" asked Bob, jacking up into a sitting position.

"It was my grandmother," said Sophie.

"So, why are you crying? Is she sick?"

"She told me she needed a gallbladder operation, but I think she's dying."

Bob held up his hands in a gesture of helplessness.

"Why would you think that?"

"I could hear it in her voice," Sophie cried.

Bob was too in love with Sophie to chide her for melodrama. He took her in his arms and pulled her close.

"It's not unusual to be nervous before surgery," he reasoned. "You get nervous and your voice goes up. Right? I'll bet you she'll be just fine."

"No, I don't think so," said Sophie, pressing her face into Bob's hard, hairless chest. "I already feel her slipping away. I need to be with her. I need to go home right away."

"I'll go with you."

Sophie considered the complication of bringing Bob home. She knew her mother would be berserk with worry, even more anxious than usual to find fault. Roma couldn't be bothered with a young stranger in the house, even a well-meaning one.

Sophie said, "I appreciate your offering, but it would be better if I went alone." She kissed his lips to take some of the edge off the rejection.

Sophie got up and lifted a window shade. The dull gray sky was shedding wet snowflakes that were already sticking to the dead grass. She dragged a battered suitcase from her closet and began to fill it with winter wear. Bob watched while Sophie emptied her sweater drawer.

"How long are you planning to be away?" he asked.

"I don't know," she said, mechanically tossing in socks and flannel nightgowns. Her mind was already on the four-hour trip ahead. She wanted to get out of town before nightfall. She would not call her parents first. They would only try to discourage her from coming.

They would question her sanity for setting out in the snow for a mere gallbladder. Even a heart or a brain would be questionable cause for a late-day trip in frozen precipitation.

Sophie got dressed and laced up her boots. Bob placed a hand on her shoulder.

"Are you sure you want to go by yourself?" he asked. "I could drive down with you and take a bus back. I hate the thought of you heading out alone in a snowstorm feeling the way you do."

"I'll be all right," she said. "The Javelin knows this trip by heart."

She managed a weak smile.

"Maybe you can carry my bag out to the car."

Sophie slipped into her sports car and rolled down the window to kiss Bob good-bye.

"Be careful on the road, and call me when you get there," said Bob. "I'll take in your mail and feed your cat, don't worry."

Sophie inwardly winced at Bob's tetracycline-stained smile and wished she could love him. She touched his bearded cheek and said, "Thank you."

She watched him get smaller in the rearview mirror as she drove away on the rutted road. She knew she wouldn't call.

New York 1974

12

It was fully dark when Sophie arrived at her parent's ranch-style house in Syosset. The light snow had turned to rain just south of Hartford, but the stars shone bright on Tulip Lane. She pulled into the driveway and parked in front of the single-car garage. There were no lights on. Sophie wondered if her parents were at the hospital. She hoped they hadn't changed the locks since she was last home. She sat in the car with her hands still on the wheel, staring at her old bedroom window. The shades were drawn. Sophie extended her gaze to take in the whole house.

The Gordons had moved to the house on Tulip Lane when Sophie was six. Coming from the apartment in Flushing, the new house was palatial. The living room had a gold cathedral ceiling and flocked wallpaper like an upscale bordello. Downstairs from the living room was a wet bar, where Bill kept his prized bottle of Chivas Regal scotch. The bottle was older than Sophie and she suspected it was still half-full, even with the few nips she sneaked every time she visited. The Gordons weren't big drinkers.

Sophie's room had a shocking-pink carpet that matched a floral wallpaper so loud that flowers morphed into sailors and dancing dogs in the dark, discouraging Sophie's childhood friends from spending the night. There were twin beds in the room and Gram stayed with her when she visited. Gram wasn't afraid of the wallpaper.

Gabe slept in a twin bed in Ron's burnt-orange room. The walls in the house were very thin. When Ida and Gabe visited, everybody rushed to fall asleep quickly before Gabe started to snore.

Sophie hardly ever slept, with or without snoring. She suffered from night terrors, aggravated by the suspenseful strains of the *Perry*

Mason theme or, worse yet, Boris Karloff hosting *Thriller*. The cherry-red TV room was right across the narrow hallway from Sophie's room and the sound easily passed through the plasterboard. Sophie trembled in her bed and thought about death, when it would come and whom it would take.

Hours after her bedtime, the TV was finally shut off and Bill would stand in the shadow of Sophie's doorway, checking on her. She knew the hulking gray outline was her father, but the sensation of being silently observed was almost as frightening as her brother groaning in his sleep on the other side of the wall.

"I can't sleep," Sophie whimpered from somewhere deep inside her disheveled nest of blankets. She poked her head through when Bill came into her room and sat on the edge of her bed. Bill wiggled his fingers in front of his daughter's wide eyes and in a deep, hypnotic voice intoned, "Sleeeeeep."

"It's not working, Daddy." Sophie slipped back into her cocoon. "I'm scared," she said.

Bill stopped waving his hands and asked, "What are you afraid of, sweetheart?"

"I keep seeing everybody I love lined up in boxes. Promise me you'll never die."

Bill wondered when Sophie would outgrow her fear of death. He decided to distract her with a story.

"You know, I am not from this place," he said.

"What place, Daddy?"

"Earth."

"You mean you're from a different planet?"

Sophie could almost hear Boris Karloff rasping, "This is going to be a '*twiller*'".

"That is correct," said Bill in a metallic voice. "I am not from this planet. I am here by day. At night, I travel across the galaxy. And, you know what else?"

Sophie was afraid to ask but ventured a quavering "What?"

"You are not of this place either. Have you noticed our skin coloring? We are green. In fact, my mother was a Green."

"Wasn't that her name before she married Grandpa Joseph?"

"Yes, sweetheart. We come from a long line of Greens."

Sophie had heard this story many times. When she was much older, she would ask her father, "Jesus Christ, Dad, why did you use to give me that crock of shit about us being aliens? We aren't green, we're olive, and we're olive because we we're Jews, not Martians." But at six, she wondered where her father traveled to at night and if she, too, would someday take flight.

One sleepless night, Sophie soundlessly peaked into her parents' moonlit purple bedroom and watched her father standing in front of his window staring at the heavens. The sky appeared striped with deep red and yellow jet streams. Bill stood motionless like an empty husk in boxer shorts. Roma slept soundly on her side of the bed, buried under covers humped like a tortoise shell. Neither parent seemed reachable. Sophie withdrew to her own room, six feet away, and shuddered in the dark, waiting for morning to come.

A light went on in the front of the house and shook Sophie out of her reverie. It had gotten cold in the car. Sophie got out and stretched her legs before getting her suitcase out of the trunk. As she approached the amber-glass-encased entry, her father stood waiting for her behind the screened door. He was wearing a James Bond-style maroon smoking jacket over his underwear and worn-out leather slippers. Bill Gordon was not a smoker.

"Sophie, sweetheart, what a wonderful surprise!" he said, giving his daughter a tight hug. "We weren't expecting you. Is everything all right?"

Roma came into the golden living room dressed in a flowered kimono and woolen socks. "Sophie! What are you doing here?" she asked.

Sophie could hear Senor Wences in the background. It was around eight-thirty on Sunday evening and the *Ed Sullivan Show* was on.

"Grandma called me."

"What did she call *you* for?" asked Roma.

"What do you think?" asked Sophie.

You didn't need to come running home," Roma said.

She rummaged for a pack of cigarettes in the deep pocket of her kimono.

"But I did, Ma."

"Well then, come on in. We have to get up early in the morning and head over to the hospital."

Bill was already carrying Sophie's suitcase into her room. Sophie removed her boots and walked up the stairs in her socks. She took Roma in a bear hug, careful to avoid the lit cigarette in Roma's hand, and kissed her on both cheeks. "Mwaa, mwaa," went the smacker. Roma kissed her back and said, "I'm glad you're home. Grandma doesn't look good to me. She's all yellow."

At least she's not green, thought Sophie.

"It sounds like she might be jaundiced," she said.

"We'll know more tomorrow," said Roma. "Did you eat? I could toast you a bagel."

"That sounds good. I haven't eaten since I spoke with Grandma this afternoon."

"What did she say to you?" asked Roma.

"She said she was having gallbladder surgery. It was a short conversation. "Where's Grandpa?"

"At your Aunt Lenore's. She's taking him to the hospital in the morning."

Sophie sat at the gray Formica table in the turquoise-flowered kitchen while Roma pulled a bag of bagels from the freezer. The bagels had been pre-sliced and were thin enough to fit in the toaster. Sophie felt exhaustion hit her as she sank into a chair. Its pneumatic cushion emitted a rude hiss. Bill came into the kitchen and sat across from her. He placed a hand on hers and said, "So, how's my favorite daughter? It's such a delight to have you home. I've missed you."

Sophie squeezed his hand and said, "I've missed you, too."

Roma slammed a browned bagel in a Corel plate on the table, making Bill, Sophie and the bagel jump. She was gentler with the knife and cream cheese. Roma squirted Sophie a glass of seltzer from a blue siphon bottle and announced she was going back into the den to finish watching her show before going to bed. She gave Sophie another rough kiss, and left in a puff of cigarette smoke and a whiff of burnt bread.

Bill shifted in his seat, at a loss for words. His daughter was twenty-one and fully-grown, a leggy beauty with a sultry look.

"Was there a lot of traffic on the road?" he asked.

"Not much. At least I didn't have to deal with rush hour."

"How was the weather?"

"It was snowing in Boston when I left, but just barely."

Sophie spoke between bites. Her father looked comical in his smoking jacket sitting with his hairy legs primly crossed. Sophie supposed he felt very much at home without his trousers. She wondered with a goofy smile if this was acceptable attire for nocturnal space travel. She was still grinning when she asked, "Is Gram going to be all right, Dad?"

"Sure darling, why not? Her gallbladder's been acting up, that's all. You didn't need to come all the way home, but I always love to have you here."

Bill patted Sophie's hand.

"You must be exhausted. I put your bag in your room. Why don't you try to get some rest? What time do you want me to wake you up in the morning?"

"What time do we have to leave for the hospital?"

"The operation's scheduled for ten. We should leave here by eight-thirty. Grandma's already there. Your aunt took her this afternoon."

"Can I call Grandma now?"

Bill looked at his watch. It was after nine.

"I wouldn't, sweetheart. She may be asleep already. Maybe you'll be able to see her in the morning, if we get there early enough. What time do you want to wake up? Five?"

Bill was an early bird.

Sophie narrowed her eyes and said, "Do you really think I need three-and-a-half hours to get ready?"

Bill shrugged and said, "I don't know how long you need. Mother's a slow riser."

Sophie chuckled at the understatement. Roma was usually turning over on her left side at ten. She was a marathon sleeper.

Sophie got up to rinse off her plate and put away the cream cheese. There was no dishwashing liquid and no sponge. She sprinkled the plate with Ajax cleanser and rubbed it under the tap with her bare hands. Her fingerprints felt scrubbed off. She could now commit the perfect crime.

"How about waking me at seven-thirty, Dad? That should give me all the time I need."

Bill grabbed a handful of filberts from the pantry and said, "I'll set my mental alarm. Mom is probably already in bed. Her show is over. See you in the morning, sweetheart."

Bill kissed his daughter on the cheek and ambled down the hall to his bedroom, his mouth full of nuts. When his door closed, Sophie sneaked down to the basement and had a shot of Chivas, straight from the bottle.

13

Sophie stood at the entrance of her old bedroom and flicked the wall switch. The light that came on was mercifully dim. The pink carpet had been replaced with an avocado one when she turned thirteen. At the same time, the frightful flowered wallpaper was buried beneath a more subdued harvest gold and avocado stripe. Sophie could still visualize the sailors and dancing dogs.

Bill's mother, Rose, had died a few years before and some of her furniture had found its way into Sophie's bedroom. Sophie had never been close to Grandma Rose, the former Green. Rose was an elegant but cold woman. Her cashmere and mink sweaters were lined up in Sophie's closet and smelled of lavender, but Sophie found no comfort in their touch or scent.

Rose's furniture gave Sophie's room an air of European sophistication. There was a sleek white desk and matching chair with a creamy green seat cushion and a white dresser in a corner of the room upon which Sophie formerly housed her dime-store turtles in their glass aquarium with the plastic palm tree in the middle.

Sophie walked into the room and lifted the window shade. She saw the dreaded water tower beacon that had contributed to her night terrors. For years, Sophie was convinced there were little silver aliens in the tower, perhaps distant relatives. She smirked at the memory. The theme from *The Twilight Zone* played in her head.

Sophie selected an outfit for the following morning and laid it out on the twin bed opposite her own. She shrugged her shoulders against the day's fatigue. After washing up in the canary-yellow bathroom where she and Ron had water fights and escaped from Roma's rages, Sophie pulled back the gold comforter and slipped onto a cold, stale, checkered sheet. She removed her eyeglasses and clicked off the table lamp. She stared into the dark, wide-awake and half-blind.

"Well, here I am," she whispered.

Sophie had always spoken aloud to herself in this bed to get her through the long, sleepless nights of her childhood.

"I haven't been home in a long time," she said to the low ceiling. "I'm here because my grandmother's sick. Of everyone else in the world, she's the one I fear losing the most. Please take care of her and keep her safe."

Sophie ended her entreaty with a silent "Amen," and then turned abruptly on her side, embarrassed by her piety.

As always, sleep wouldn't come. The clock beside her bed relentlessly ticked the hours away. A streetlamp kept the room a dim gray. Suddenly, Sophie became aware of a presence. She felt a tightening in her chest where her ribs met. She propped herself up on her elbow and stared at the outline of a large figure in the left-hand corner of her room.

Fear constricted her throat. If she were able to utter any sound at all, she was going to have to scream it, loudly enough to wake her father, loudly enough to wake the dead. What if she screamed and her father didn't come? Sophie opened her mouth wide but lost the power to engage her vocal cords. She was mildly relieved that she wouldn't have to hear herself shriek. She closed her eyes, hoping that when she opened them, the shadowed presence would be gone.

Sophie braced herself and fluttered an eyelid. With great speed, the hulk was no longer in a blurry corner. His face was in clear focus right before her now wide-open eyes. He came at her like a comet, with wild hair and gaping mouth. His gaze burned into her and knocked her back against her pillow with tremendous force. Sophie lay panting, with her legs writhing against the coarse, damp sheet until consciousness fled and blackness came. Sophie finally slept and, within sleep, a former life presented itself in vivid clarity.

Sophie recognized the house at once. It was a dimly lit two-story hovel with lots of people living in it. Ida was there as a young woman.

Her bobbed hair was black and her natural teeth were long. She was wearing woolen knickers and thick knee socks. Gabe was holding an infant with blond curls. He was very thin. He wore baggy pants and suspenders over a ribbed undershirt. Ida's three sisters were there with their husbands. Two older children were banging on the piano in the parlor. A crippled border was hobbling up the stairs one step at a time on his peg leg.

There was a commotion in the kitchen. Nana Sofia was standing over Zayde Gershon, threatening him with a frying pan. They looked like a Slavic version of *Andy Capp*.

Gershon was sitting at the kitchen table with his head in his hands. A shot glass of vodka was within his reach. Sofia was shouting in Russian, "How could you gamble all our money away, you drunken hooligan? How am I going to feed this family with no money?"

Gershon looked up at Sofia with bloodshot eyes and shook his head.

Sofia looked like a cross between Mrs. Kruschev and Jack Oakie. Two thick braids connected at the top of her head, exposing a plain, round face. Gershon's face looked skeletal in comparison, worn thin with depravity and remorse. He turned away from his wife and wept.

"There are fourteen people living in this house," shouted Sofia. "Do you know what we're eating tonight? *Lokshen*! Is that a meal for fourteen people?" Sofia ladled out a bowl of noodles and dumped it on Gershon's head. "There! There is your portion!"

The crowded house fell silent. The only sound was the lum-pum, lum-pum of the one-legged border inching his way up the stairs.

Gershon sat with noodles streaming down his face onto the kitchen table.

"What do you have to say for yourself?" shrieked Sofia, the frying pan back in her hand.

Gershon took a soiled handkerchief from his pocket and wiped his eyes. With a shaking hand, he reached for the shot glass and downed the vodka. "That's the end of it," he said, slapping the glass back down on the table.

Sofia plucked a few stray noodles out of her husband's hair and kissed his head. "I want to believe you," she said. She took a few coins from her purse and held them out to him. "Here," she said, "go buy bananas and cream and candy for the children. Tonight, the Polokovs will have something other than noodles to eat."

Sophie awoke with a taste of wintergreen in her mouth. Her father was knocking on her door saying, "It's seven-thirty." She didn't have to look at the clock to know that it was seven-thirty on the nose.

14

Sophie and her parents piled into Bill's Chrysler and headed to the hospital. It was a cold day with a sharp, cutting wind. Roma was buried in her antique Persian lamb coat, which Sophie now coveted. She sat hunched over in the passenger seat, dowsed in perfume and hairspray and smoking her Newports. Sophie gagged in the back seat, begging her mother to allow her to open her window a crack.

"I don't want my hair to blow," said Roma.

"Your hair isn't going anywhere," said Sophie. "It's stiff as a board. In the meantime, I'm suffocating. Put out the cigarette, at least."

"Don't bother me now with the cigarettes, Sophie."

"I knew I should've taken my own car," Sophie muttered.

"What do you need your own car for?" asked Bill.

"Because I can breath in my own car."

"You sound very nervous, Sophie," said Bill. "Why don't you calm down?"

"Because I'm struggling for breath. Do me a favor. Will you drop me off at the emergency room? I'm going to need an iron lung."

"Oh, for God's sake. Roma, we need to open a window."

Roma viciously crushed the life out of her Newport in the ashtray and screamed, "There, the cigarette is out. Are you happy now?"

A halo of smoke engulfed her embalmed bouffant as she sat fuming in the front seat, her bottom lip poking out.

They sat in silence as the car crawled along in rush hour traffic. Sophie pressed her forehead against the cool window, fighting nausea, as she looked out on the boxy Cape Cods, ranches and split-levels of western Long Island. Even with traffic congestion, it was a short ride to the hospital—a one-fight trip. Bill dropped Roma and Sophie at the entrance and went off to find a parking space.

Sophie left Roma smoking at the front door and went up to the information desk to find out which room her grandmother was in.

The attendant looked through a file and said, "She's in room five sixty-seven, but I think she's being prepped, honey."

"Can I go up and check?"

"Sure. The elevator is on the right. Take it to the fifth floor and turn left."

Sophie looked through the double glass doors and saw that Roma was still smoking, blowing out plumes of smoke and frosty mist, waiting for Bill. She took this opportunity to have a few moments alone with her grandmother. Sophie slipped into an elevator crowded with doctors in blue, skinny candy stripers with magazine carts and visitors still shedding chilliness from their coats. When she got off on the fifth floor, she ran directly into her aunt Lenore and grandfather.

"Look who's here," said Lenore, rearing back for a better look. "Have you lost weight?"

"No, I guess I'm just getting haggard," said Sophie, giving her aunt a hug. "Hi Grandpa," she said, squeezing him tightly in her arms.

"Hi, sweetheart," said Gabe. "Are you here alone?"

"No, my father's out parking the car and my mother's waiting for him."

"Smoking up a storm, I'll bet," said Lenore.

"That's right," said Sophie. "Have you seen Grandma yet?"

"No, we just got here ourselves," said Lenore.

"You mind if I run in and speak with Gram alone for a minute?"

"Go on ahead. We'll wait for your parents."

Sophie scurried down the hall and saw that the door labeled "Weiss" was partially ajar. There were two beds in the room, separated by a partition. Nobody was occupying the first bed. Sophie knocked on the door and said, "Gram?"

"Sophie," said Ida from the other side of the screen. "Over here. Come in."

Sophie bounded into the room and stopped short when she saw her grandmother. "So this is where they've hidden you," she joked.

Sophie bent to kiss Ida's yellowed cheek and sat at the edge of the bed, careful to avoid the intravenous tube weaving its way into Ida's arm. Sophie took Ida's hand and the two women meshed fingers. Sophie noted with relief that her grandmother's grip was as strong as ever. Maybe death wasn't lurking in the shadows, after all.

"You look a little pale," said Ida, looking up at Sophie's face. Her eyes looked huge behind her glasses.

"I'm fine," said Sophie. "How are *you* feeling?"

"Lousy. I feel like I've swallowed poison."

"I understand that a bum gallbladder can make you feel that way."

"I feel like I'm going to die."

Sophie's knees buckled and she clutched the metal headboard for support. Her moment of rosy optimism went up in smoke. "Oh, Gram, you're not going to die," Sophie said.

She silently cursed herself for sounding so unconvincing. Ida let it pass.

"I hope not, sweetheart," she said. "I'm so happy that you came down to see me."

"Of course, I came down. And, I'll be here when you wake up. And, I'll be here to take you home."

Sophie clenched Ida's hand and felt the beginning of a terrible loss. Gram's face was the first she had ever seen as she lingered between life and death shortly after her birth. Sophie was a RH baby, and the survivor of an experimental blood transfusion. In the ten days she spent in intensive care, only her grandmother had come to see her. Roma stayed away, content to sleep alone in her cozy hospital bed.

Sophie looked at her grandmother's eyes now and knew that Ida was closer to death than to life. She felt like saying, "Don't leave me," but came out with "Don't worry." Their hands gripped tightly.

Sophie heard voices approaching. Her family was coming, along with an entourage of professionals. The professionals would cart Grandma Ida away, leaving the family to wring their hands and embrace in the hallway, whispering words of encouragement into necks still cold from the street. When Ida had been transferred to a gurney and secured, Sophie kissed her and whispered, "I love you. I'll see you soon."

Ida nodded and closed her eyes. She smiled peacefully, her hand now lying flat across her heart. Sophie couldn't bear to look at it.

15

The surgeon came into the waiting room earlier than expected. Roma and Lenore began whimpering as soon as they saw the expression on his face. He addressed them directly. "We opened her up and closed her right back. Your mother's got advanced liver cancer. I'm afraid she doesn't have much time left. I'm very sorry."

Roma started a long wail that ended in an anguished, "Mama's got cancer."

The word "cancer" came out a ragged scream. Lenore ran to attend to her father who had paled and collapsed in his chair. A nurse was summoned to revive him. Bill tried in vain to calm his wife, strangling her grief in his arms.

Sophie calmly took a cigarette and lighter from her mother's purse and rode the elevator to the hospital lobby. She had left her parka in the waiting room. As she walked through the glass doors into the now-gray afternoon, the frigid air felt good. She turned away from the wind and lit the cigarette, inhaling deeply. Her throat began to burn but she sucked on the cigarette like it was oxygen and she was drowning. Soon it was all used up. She didn't know what to do with her hands. She shoved them into her armpits and watched the swirl of traffic at the hospital entrance. Her head felt like a block of ice.

A dark-haired stranger in a midnight-blue suit was suddenly beside her, taking a pack of Kools from his breast pocket. He shook a cigarette from the pack and asked, "Would you like one of mine?"

"Yes, please," she said, looking into the man's colorless eyes. Her gaze lingered there, and Sophie felt a strange heat spread through her body like a bloodstain.

The stranger lit the cigarette and placed it between her lips. He took the spent butt from her hand and crushed it out under his heel. Sophie swallowed the menthol smoke and felt a cold blast coursing through her lungs. She closed her eyes and felt the tears seep out, hot against her frosty cheeks.

Somebody put a coat over her shoulders.

"Are you all right, sweetheart?" asked her father. "We didn't know where you had taken off to. Why are you smoking?"

"I don't know," said Sophie, putting the cigarette behind her back. She looked around for the man in the blue suit but he was no longer there.

"Come back inside," Bill said. It's cold out here."

"Give me a minute," said Sophie. "Thanks for bringing the coat down. I'll be right up."

"Why don't you come with me?"

"Because I want to be alone for a minute."

Sophie was anxious to put the cigarette back in her mouth but didn't want to ruin the experience with one of her father's health lectures. She was desperate to puff in private and fretted that the cigarette would burn itself out.

"Dad, if you don't leave right now, I'm going to smoke an entire carton of cigarettes out of every orifice in my body. I'm going to swallow a gallon of scotch. I'm going to snort a barrel of cocaine. Please, for Christ's sake, leave me alone for a few more minutes."

Sophie glared until Bill took the hint.

"Come up soon," he said. "I don't want you to catch a cold."

As soon as Bill was out of sight, Sophie took a deep drag and held it in her lungs. When she opened her mouth, the pale blue smoke burst out like a shout. Sophie realized that the dreaded coffins of her youth were beginning to fill. She danced from one foot to the other like Hiawatha imploring the gods for rain and thought about the stranger.

Sophie was taken with him. There was something so familiar about him. Had she met him before? Had she heard his voice in her dreams? Had she slept with him in high school? Even his taste on her cigarette was recognizable. Sophie drew in on the last of the Kool and prepared to head back up to her grandmother's room. She stubbed out the cigarette, carefully wrapped its remains in a tissue and placed it in her coat pocket.

The stranger watched Sophie from a distance and smiled. He enjoyed the care she took to preserve their fleeting connection. He had implanted himself in her mind, lapping gently at her most primitive memories. He knew that she would awake each day with him in her thoughts and lull herself to sleep with dreams of him at night. Between sleeping and waking, the dreams would be rich, informing her of a reunion she was not yet willing to grasp. The stranger had waited a long time, but was infinitely patient. Sophie would soon be ready to receive him and the gifts he brought.

16

On Ida's last day, Sophie lay beside her in the hospital bed. It was a bright day, with a new layer of snow on the grass flanking the parking lot. When Sophie squeezed her grandmother's hand, she did not receive the usual squeeze in return. She opened her eyes in alarm and saw Ida's eyes peering back.

"You're awake," said Sophie.

She marveled that Ida's face was completely free of wrinkles.

"I've been watching you sleep," said Ida. "It was like you were a baby again. You sleep very quietly. If I didn't feel your breath on my face, I would wonder if you were breathing at all."

"How do you feel?" Sophie asked. Ida's voice was back to normal and Sophie allowed herself an instant to pray for a miracle.

"Never better,'" said Ida, smiling broadly.

Sophie fought back tears. Ida's mouth had been ruined by two useless chemo treatments. The smile exposed open wounds in her gums, dashing Sophie's hopes.

Ida stroked Sophie's face and kissed her on the forehead. "I have always loved you, my little Sophie," she said. "I will love you forever. Let me hold you in my arms a while."

Sophie shifted her weight on the narrow hospital bed and placed her head on the soothing fullness of her grandmother's chest. Ida stroked her granddaughter's hair and sang her a Russian lullaby. Sophie did not recognize the song.

Ida's heartbeat became erratic against Sophie's ear. When Sophie tried to spring away to get help, her grandmother held her firmly in her grasp, whispering the final words of the lullaby. Sophie suddenly understood the soft, rustling words crooned in Russian.

The child becomes a child becomes a child
She sleeps and wakes
Carried in the arms of an old love
That never leaves

Nestled in Ida's arms, Sophie began to sleep and dream. She envisioned that she was with her grandmother at an art show. Ida took her by the hand and led her to an exhibit. A man with curly dark hair and glossy black wings was on display. Sophie was drawn to the spectacle. Even without the blue suit, she could clearly see that the birdman was the stranger she had met at the entrance of the hospital. The man asked her if she was curious.

"Yes," she said.

He extended a leathery arm and invited her to feel it. "Curious?" he asked again. "Yes," she said.

The creature bent and kissed Sophie on the lips. Spreading his wings wide, he flew from his pedestal. Ida's voice was in her head now.

"His name is Gershon and he is your intended," she said.

Sophie woke up and lay in her grandmother's arms with her eyes closed. Ida's body was cool and still and yet, even in death, Sophie could still feel her love. She didn't hasten to rise, dreading the hysteria that would soon break out, with doctors and nurses sprinting to and fro in rubber-soled shoes and family members screaming to wake the dead. She selfishly relished having Ida to herself for a few more precious moments. Encased so lovingly in her grandmother's embrace, Sophie enjoyed the illusion that Ida still lived.

Massachusetts 1974

17

As Sophie drove back to Boston, a January thaw was melting the dirty snow. Sophie dangled a cigarette out the car window. She had snatched a few of her mother's Newports, along with a packet of matches from Hong's House of Fortune. She caught a glimpse of herself inhaling in the side-view mirror and cringed at the lines that formed around her mouth as she sucked on the soggy brown filter. Sophie flicked the butt into oncoming traffic.

Donna Summer was moaning, *"I love to love you, baby"* on Ten Ten WINS and Sophie began to squirm in her seat. Pushing her hips forward in time to the music, Sophie pressed a finger against the hard seam between her legs and her insides clenched. She wanted to get back to Brighton before nightfall, but an urge to pull over sidelined her intentions. She was desperate to stop, like a woman on the verge of giving birth is desperate to get to a hospital before she has to use a cab driver's shoulders as stirrups. Sophie needed release, but not at eighty-five miles per hour on the New England Thruway.

Sophie stopped at a nearly deserted rest stop in southern Connecticut and ran into the empty ladies room. She locked herself into a stall and yanked her jeans down over her hips. She conjured up the blue-suited stranger from the hospital and actually felt as if she were mounted on his solid thighs, kissing his mint-flavored mouth.

Sophie worked quickly with her fingers, alert for sounds of civilization. She could feel the stranger's breath against her face and lurched forward, driven to grasp the fine hair on his muscular chest. Sophie's eyes fluttered and she took a great intake of breath just before a mother came crashing into the bathroom with at least two wailing children. After releasing a shuddering sigh into her coat sleeve, Sophie wiped up the wetness between her legs and waited for the harried mother to tend to her babies and leave.

As her heart rate settled down, the potty talk from the stall next door got her mind back to getting home before dark. As soon as the coast was clear, Sophie washed her hands and sauntered out to her car. She figured one more cigarette wouldn't slow her down that much. She lit one and blew wisps of smoke into the fetid air of Bridgeport, leaning against her Javelin. She wondered, fleetingly, if Bob would be angry with her for not calling.

The question answered itself the minute it was posed. Sophie had never seen Bob angry. He was entirely tame, she realized with a small twinge of regret. His timidity ignited a strange cruelty in her. She sometimes felt like telling him to put up his dukes. On the other hand, she had come to rely upon his calm demeanor. He was her shelter in a storm. Suddenly, she was most anxious to see him. She couldn't wait to wrap her arms around his lean waist. Sophie ground out her cigarette and hopped into her car, bidding a fond farewell to the rest stop of her dreams.

Sophie arrived home by twilight. Her various roommates and their boyfriends were scattered about like mismatched socks. She received pats and kisses when they learned of her loss and then they all withdrew back into their corners. Sophie lifted the receiver in the kitchen and called Bob, who answered on the first ring.

"Were you expecting me?" asked Sophie.

"Yes, weeks ago," said Bob. "Why didn't you call me?"

Bob actually sounded agitated, for Bob. Especially when he added, "I was worried, damn it."

"Why didn't you call *me*, then?" asked Sophie.

"I did," he said. "I wanted to give you some space but needed to know if you were dead or alive. I just got off the phone with your father. I'm very sorry about your grandmother, Sophie."

Sophie felt a sudden weariness and leaned against the counter.

"Thank you, Bobby," she said, enjoying the sound of his nickname.

"It was good that I went home. Gram knew before anyone else that she was dying."

"She needed to know you would be all right with that," said Bob.

"I will never be all right with that, but, in the end, I needed to release her. I've taken up smoking, by the way."

Bob was a two-pack-a-day man himself.

"Good," he said. "So you won't mind if I blow smoke in your hair."

"Just don't blow it up my ass."

Sophie giggled at her crassness.

Bob chuckled with her and said, "I missed you, Sophie. May I come over and share your pillow?"

Sophie grimaced at Bob's Shakespearean request but said, "My pillow is your pillow."

Sophie envisioned that, tonight, Bob would be an innocent lamb and she would be a ravaging lion. She couldn't wait for him to expose the tender underside of his throat so she could slash it with her tongue. Sophie shook the horrid image from her mind, wondering where it had come from.

She went into her room and found it as she'd left it, with the curtains drawn and the bed unmade. She hastened to change the linens and freshen the air. She opened one stiff window and smiled when she saw a full moon rising. The cat came in and nudged her legs.

"Oh, Rex, I nearly forgot about you," she said, lifting the squirming creature over her head. "Did everybody take good care of you while Mommy was away?"

Rex meowed plaintively and swatted Sophie softly on the nose. Sophie put the cat down and said, "Guess who's coming over? Bob. That means Mommy's got to take a shower and put on something slutty."

Rex ran out of the room.

"I was only kidding," Sophie called after the fleeing cat.

Sophie rummaged through her lingerie drawer. She ran her hands over a lacy merry widow but wasn't in the mood to fuss with snaps and garters. She selected a sleek pink satin sheath and a silver arm bracelet shaped like a poised cobra. She found a clean towel in her closet and headed into the bathroom. She was grateful to discover it was empty for a change.

Sophie flipped several damp towels off the shower rod and placed them in the sink. The room was still humid from recent use. She undressed in front of the large mirror that hovered over the toothpaste-splattered sink. When she sucked in her stomach, her ribs stood out like staves and her breasts looked larger than her head. Sophie tried not to focus on her face. She thought her nose was too big and her eyes were too small. She sighed and stepped into the tub and was relieved that the porcelain was still warm.

Sophie turned on the water and stood in a tepid weak stream, one of the perils of sharing plumbing with seven others. She frantically pushed the shampoo out of her hair and quickly soaped and rinsed her body before the water went dead cold. Sophie leaped out of the tub and toweled herself briskly. She combed the knots out of her hair and strategically dabbed at herself with honeysuckle perfume. She installed her medieval diaphragm and slithered into her dainty slip. Sophie felt herself ovulate with anticipation. Maybe *she* would be the lamb tonight.

Her room felt like the frozen tundra. Sophie ran to the open window and slammed it shut, snapping the curtains together. She lay shivering in her clean bed, beneath her fluffy quilt, waiting for Bob and his warm body to arrive.

18

Bob took Sophie to meet his parents on New Year's Day. The Sterns lived in a Cape Cod in Malden, where they raised Bob and his three older sisters. The house was already a relic when they bought it thirty years before. Winter weeds grew through cracks in the cement path leading to the front door, but the pathway was lined with neatly-trimmed forsythia. Bob pointed to a dormer window with navy shutters and said, "That was my room growing up." Sophie noticed that the blinds were open.

Bob used his key to open the door and ushered Sophie into the dark, lemon-scented foyer. Somewhere, a television blared. A tall grandfather clock stood against the brown wall, its pendulum swaying ponderously. Sophie took Bob by the arm and asked, "Why is it so dark in here?"

"Mom is visually impaired."

"Would turning on a lamp help?"

Bob laughed and said, "It would help us, but it wouldn't do much for her. She's blind as a bat. No need to waste electricity on light."

"What about your father?"

"He knows his way around. Unfortunately, his hearing is going."

"Didn't you tell me your father was a professional musician?"

"Yes. Lucky for him, he's got a day job, selling appliances at Lechmere's."

Bob took Sophie by the hand and led her into the dim living room, where his silver-haired father was perched in a recliner in front of a small TV set watching a football game. He jumped up when he saw his son. "Bobby!" he shouted, "I didn't hear you come in. Welcome! Evelyn, Bobby's here and he's brought a lovely friend."

Bob's mother rose from the maroon velour couch and stood in place with her arms outstretched like a condemned prisoner pleading for a stay of execution. "Oh, Bobby," she said, "please bring her over here."

Bobby hugged his mother and said, "Mom and Dad, I'd like to introduce you to Sophie."

With her high cheekbones and smooth, pale skin, Mrs. Stern was still a delicate beauty. She wore a flowered shirtwaist and a pink angora cardigan. Her luminous blue eyes stared into the space above Sophie's head.

"How do you do, dear," she said. "How nice it is to meet you. Bobby has told us so much about you. We were so sorry to hear about your grandmother."

She lifted her hands and Bob guided them to Sophie's cheeks.

"Do you mind if I look at you?" she asked.

"Not at all," said Sophie, noticing how much Bob resembled his mother. Mrs. Stern gently slid her cool fingers around the curves and angles of Sophie's face and said, "Aren't you a pretty one."

"She sure is," yelled Mr. Stern over the TV. "She's got your coloring, Evelyn. Doesn't she, Bobby?"

"Well, yes, now that you mention it," said Bob uncomfortably. "Dad, why don't we all sit down? Can we turn down the TV so we can hear each other?"

"Sure, son." Mr. Stern ambled over to the TV and turned the volume knob counterclockwise. "Is that better?" he asked. "I can't hear a damn thing anymore. Would anybody like a sandwich?"

"We already ate, Dad, but thanks."

"How about a cup of coffee and a piece of marble pound cake, then? It's already perked and sliced. We can have it right here in the living room."

"That sounds perfect, Mr. Stern," said Sophie.

"She's got your sweet tooth, Evelyn," he shouted, running toward the kitchen.

Mrs. Stern clapped her hands in front of her upturned nose like a girl and said, "Oh Fred, show me a woman who doesn't love sweets."

Locating Sophie's hand, Mrs. Stern sat back down on the sofa, taking Sophie with her. "Bobby doesn't bring just anyone home," she said. "We hope that we'll be seeing more of you. Bobby tells us you're studying psychology. Are you planning on becoming a therapist? Maybe you can analyze me."

Sophie laughed and said, "Well, yes, maybe someday. I have to warn you, though—I come from a long line of psych majors. We end up selling real estate."

"Oh, that's all right, dear. We could just have a chat now and then and I could tell you all my little secrets. I hardly ever hear from my own daughters anymore. They're all gone, leading their grown-up lives. Bobby's the only one left who's still within driving distance. He's a joy to have around."

"What kind of little secrets do you have, Ma?" asked Bob, winking at Sophie. "Have you been slipping out with the mailman again?"

Mrs. Stern smiled and said, "Oh, nothing like that, dear."

"I'd be happy to talk to you whenever you'd like," said Sophie, wondering if Mrs. Stern was truly blind.

Mr. Stern bustled into the living room with a big metal tray. Coffee cups leaped when the tray hit the walnut coffee table. "Refreshments are being served," he announced enthusiastically.

Sophie was impressed with the repast Mr. Stern had assembled. Not only did the tray hold the promised coffee and cake, but also ginger snaps, chocolate-covered almonds and glistening dried apricots. Cream and sugar were presented in elegant crystal containers. The gilded china was Wedgewood and Sophie suspected that the ornate but tasteful flatware was sterling.

Sophie said," What a wonderful feast! You've gone to a lot of trouble."

"No trouble at all, sweetheart. Nothing's too good for my son and his lovely friend. Can I call her your girlfriend, Bobby?"

Bob and Sophie exchanged glances. Sophie nodded and Bob said, "Yes, Dad, Sophie's my girlfriend."

Bob lifted Sophie's face by the chin and kissed her lightly on the lips. He looked both baffled and elated.

"Terrific. In that case, call me Fred, Sophie. Mr. Stern was my father."

"What are you planning to do when you graduate, Sophie?" asked Mrs. Stern.

"I haven't decided yet. If I truly want to practice psychology, I'll need to go on to graduate school."

"Bobby's going to law school. I hope you get accepted into schools in the same city. Maybe you'll both get into Harvard. Then, you'll be right down the block."

"Let's not get ahead of ourselves, Evelyn," said Mr. Stern, handing her a cup of coffee with a splash of cream.

"Do you have brothers or sisters?" asked Mrs. Stern.

"I have an older brother in Montana."

"Oh, how exciting to live in the mountains. I've never been out of the northeast. Fred and I got married straight out of high school and we began our family early. Bobby was still in junior high when I began losing my vision. Glaucoma. I see shadows every once in a while, but I can't tell a cat from a coconut. I'm so lucky to have a good husband. He does everything for me. Bobby's a good man like his father."

"Thanks, Ma," said Bob stroking her thin shoulder.

"Do you want children, Sophie?" asked Mrs. Stern.

Bob and his father simultaneously squawked, "Ma!" "Evelyn!"

Sophie lifted a hand to quiet them and said, "I haven't thought much about it, Mrs. Stern. Maybe. I just don't know yet. I'm open to it."

"Don't wait too long, dear. The years have a tendency to run away. One day, you'll wake up and you'll be forty and it'll be too late."

"I'll keep that in mind," Sophie said.

Bob was looking miserably into his open palms, like he was reading a sad book. Sophie pressed a chocolate nut into his down-turned mouth and helped herself to a ginger snap.

"Do you two have marriage plans?" asked Mrs. Stern.

She sat with her hands demurely in her lap, a radiant glow in her sightless eyes.

"No, Mother, we do not," said Bob, unraveling. "I just learned that Sophie was my girlfriend, for God's sake. We've only been going out for a couple of months. We have careers to think about. And, forty is nearly twenty years away."

"Calm down, Bobby," said Mr. Stern. "Here, have some cake," he said, extending a plate with a perfect wedge in the middle. Bobby took it and shoved a forkful into his mouth.

"Yes, relax, dear, I'm just making conversation," said Mrs. Stern. "I'm sure that Sophie doesn't mind. Do you, Sophie?"

"Not at all." Sophie reached out and squeezed Evelyn's cool, placid hand. She was enjoying Mrs. Stern's interest, regardless of her motives. Her own mother had always discouraged her from marrying and having children. Coming to think of it, Roma had discouraged her from having a career, too. Roma had encouraged her to be a helpless ornament.

Sophie could hear Roma now. "What do you need the piece of paper for? It's the seventies. If you like someone, live with him. Children? You want to cramp your style with sniveling brats? I wouldn't have them now if somebody paid me. Work? Why work? Play it dumb and you will always find someone to take care you. Not me, of course. I'll be out playing poker for nickels and dimes, but someone else will be happy to provide for you."

Sophie bristled at the memory.

It seemed to Sophie that Mrs. Stern was lonely for a girl to talk to, a girl who would bring her beloved son around more regularly. Evelyn's life had grown too small and she was anxious to expand it.

Maybe Sophie and Bob would live together after graduation. Perhaps they would marry. But, Sophie would never belong to Bob or any other man. She felt betrothed to a ghost who would come at a time of his own choosing. Until then, Sophie's body would produce no offspring and her soul would find no resting place. Sophie grimaced at her own silliness.

Bob would never understand.

Massachusetts 1985

19

Sophie stood in front of the bathroom mirror, inspecting her hair for gray. She plucked two strands at the temple and wondered how many years she had left before she would go bald instead of white. She swirled the dark curls onto the top of her head and secured them with a long hairclip, encrusted with faux pearls. Bob loved her hair up.

Today was Sophie's thirty-second birthday. She and Bob had been invited to her parent's house for the weekend. Roma and Bill had news. Maybe Sophie was going to get a baby sister or brother, after all. She giggled at the ridiculous thought.

Bob had a heavy caseload and would spend the trip to New York reading briefs in the passenger seat of Sophie's Mazda. Sophie had cancelled her Friday afternoon appointments, promising her most despondent patients that she would see them on Monday morning. She packed Bob's bag along with her own and was now anxious to leave.

Sophie stood at the head of the stairs of their three-story co-op in Beacon Hill and shouted, "Bob, are you going to be ready to leave anytime soon?"

The last time she'd seen him, he'd been seated at the dining room table, up to his neck in paperwork, his head attached to a phone receiver.

"Yes, babe, just give me twenty minutes and I'll be good to go."

"You told me that a half-hour ago," she said.

"What can I tell you? I'm under siege here."

"I can see that. I'll tell you what. I don't want to add to your burden. If you're not ready in twenty minutes, I'll just go without you."

Sophie hated the grinding edge to her voice, but she was tired of playing second fiddle to his work.

"Oh, for Christ's sake, be reasonable," he shouted.

Sophie ran down the winding mahogany staircase and said, "I *am* being reasonable. You agreed to go to New York with me this weekend. I've washed your clothes. I've packed your bag. I've put the mail and paper on vacation hold. I've told my patients to do without me for a day. Today, I get to drive you down to New York in silence so you can concentrate on some greedy bastard's palimony case. You've been putting me off for the past two hours. My parents expect us at six. I'm out of here at two o'clock sharp, with you or without you. Happy birthday to me."

Sophie turned on her heel and ran back up the stairs, two at a time.

Bob combed the hair out of his eyes with his fingers and pushed his chair back from the table. The chair legs squealed against the pine floor. Sophie heard him plodding slowly up the stairs as she ripped the clasp out of her hair and threw it on the unmade bed. Bob approached her from behind and gently turned her around to face him. His eyes were hooded with fatigue. Sophie tried to turn away from him, but he caught her face in his hands and kissed her hard on the mouth. Sophie's neck strained as he bore down on her and she raised her hands to his shoulders to relieve the pressure.

Bob grabbed a handful of Sophie's hair and pushed her, face-down, on the bed. While she struggled against his grasp, Sophie heard Bob unbuckling and unzipping his jeans. Sophie shouted a muffled, "Stop it" into the mattress and reared upward as Bob roughly undressed her from the waist down. Sophie reached her hands back and clawed at Bob's flank, but he captured both wrists between his long fingers and wrenched her arms up. When Sophie continued to buck, Bob slapped her hard on the buttocks with his free hand and pushed himself inside of her, without thrusting. Sophie stopped fighting as her muscles clenched around his fullness.

"What do you want?" asked Bob.

"You?" inquired Sophie, into the mattress.

"Can I let go of your hands now?" asked Bob.

"Yes."

"I don't think so," said Bob.

Retrieving his belt from the mattress, he bound Sophie's wrists behind her back. "What now?" he asked.

"What's gotten into you?" said Sophie.

She instinctively arched up against Bob's thighs.

"Nothing's gotten into me. I'm getting into you."

Bob kicked her legs apart. Plunging deeply inside of her now, Sophie felt lightheaded with pleasure. Somewhere above her, she heard Bob whispering undecipherable words as euphoria took over and brought her to a warm, white space beyond sight and sound. When she came to, Bob was lying against her back, nuzzling her hair. Both of her arms had fallen asleep, but the rest of her body felt amazingly alert.

Sophie turned her head to one side and squinted at the alarm clock. It was nearly two.

"Bobby?" she said. She almost asked, "Is that you?"

"Hmmm?"

"What in the world was that?"

"What?"

"That amazing attack."

"It was pretty amazing, wasn't it?"

"Yes," Sophie admitted, "but it was very unlike you."

"Oh, who was it like?"

"Nobody," Sophie rushed to reassure him.

"Did you like it?'

"Yes, but you're going to have to untie my hands. I can't feel them."

Sophie began to struggle against the belt that was now crushing her wrist bones. Bob's previously delightful weight was becoming a painful burden.

"Oh, Jeez," said Bob.

He catapulted himself from his wife's back and quickly released her. Sophie slowly turned over and groaned, drawing her knees to her chest. Her hands had turned an alarming shade of purple. Bob rubbed them vigorously, until Sophie dropped her legs and said, "All right, enough. Wow, I thought I'd never be able to play the violin again."

"I didn't know you played violin."

"You take me too seriously."

"Bob glanced at the clock and said, "We need to get up. We don't want to keep your parents waiting. Before we go, can you feel your hands?"

"Yes."

Bob reached into his end table and withdrew an oblong cardboard box tied with a thin gold cord.

"Happy birthday," he said, putting the box on her belly.

Sophie tilted her head forward and looked down at her stomach. The box felt oddly heavy. She wondered if it contained something garish. Pushing herself into a sitting position, Sophie untied the delicate string with tingling fingers and raised the lid. Her mouth opened when she saw the sapphire and diamond necklace and matching earrings shimmering against the black velvet lining.

"My God, Bobby, they're gorgeous!"

"They belonged to my great-grandmother," said Bob.

"I've never seen them before."

"My mother had them locked away in a vault."

"Shouldn't these go to one of your sisters?"

"No, my mother very specifically wanted you to have them. *I* want you to have them."

Sophie put her arms around Bob and said, "They're very beautiful. Did you know your great-grandmother?"

"No. She died long before I was born."

"Why did she lock them away?"

"They're very valuable. When she started raising a family, she didn't want to take a chance of losing them. You know how little girls play with their mother's belongings."

"Yes, I used to play with my mother's handkerchief collection.

She kept them in a white leather box with a hinged lid that closed to form a red heart. The handkerchiefs were always so neatly folded, and crisp, like they'd been starched. I handled them very carefully, though. I knew they were something special."

"You were unusual, then. My sisters treated my mother's precious gems like toys. They were the only possessions she had of her grandmother's. She felt the need to protect them."

"I can understand that. Why is she giving them to me now?"

"She feels like you and she share the same sensibilities about what matters in life. What have the two of you been talking about all these years?"

"She was always very interested in my ancestral background. I must admit, I never thought to ask her about hers."

"She certainly treasures you," said Bill. "My mother sees what we can't."

"I'm very honored that she chose to give me such a powerful gift. Can I wear them now?"

"They're yours. You can wear them whenever you want."

Bob was a great husband. Sophie cursed herself every time she doubted her decision to marry him. Yet, she often found herself thinking of him as a placeholder. She tried to assuage her guilt by finding fault, then feeling desperately contrite afterward.

"Sophie," said Bob, "do you think we can consider having a baby this year?"

Sophie didn't have the heart to deny him again.

"Let's talk about it on the way back from New York," she said.

New York 1985

20

We're moving to Florida," said Roma as Sophie and Bob crossed the threshold.

"What, now?" said Sophie. "I haven't even unzipped yet."

Bill rushed forward and encircled Sophie in his arms. "Hello, darling. Before you do anything, I want my kiss."

Sophie squeezed her father in a bear hug that left him groaning before he extended a hand to Bob.

"Hi, Bobby," he said. "How's my favorite son-in-law?"

"Just great, Dad. What's this I hear about you moving to Florida?"

"Yeah, what is that?" asked Sophie.

"Your father's retiring," said Roma. "It's time to sell the house and shuffle off to Boca."

"You're not old enough to do the Boca shuffle," said Sophie, copping a drag off Roma's cigarette. "Don't you have to be eighty-five to move south of Daytona?"

"Since when are you smoking?" asked Roma.

"Me? I don't smoke," said Sophie, winking at her father.

"Very smart," said Roma. "Anyway, we want you to go through your belongings and take what you want. Whatever is left behind is going into the garbage. We've already given your Barbie doll to your niece."

"Wait a minute, what are you telling me?" said Sophie. "You've already sold the house? Why didn't you discuss this with me?"

"What's there to discuss?" said Roma. "Both of you kids have been out of the house for years. I can't stand the winters here anymore and I'm bored."

"Plus I don't need the aggravation of dealing with rush hour traffic anymore," said Bill.

"That sounds reasonable," said Bob.

Sophie was going to protest but realized that Bob was right. Her parents were past sixty and their kids were grown. They no longer needed a four-bedroom house across the street from an elementary school. They needed a condo on a golf course with a clubhouse and a card room. Of course, they should move to a nice warm place with palm trees. But, why did they give away her Barbie doll? Maybe they had written off the possibility she would ever have a daughter—or a stylish son—of her own.

"Why do I feel like a middle-aged woman, all of a sudden?" Sophie asked.

"What are you talking about, sweetheart?" asked Bill. "You've got years to go before you're middle-aged."

"It's just that if you are moving into retirement, it seems like I have to move into a new phase myself. Adulthood comes to mind."

"What then?" Roma asked. "You're a big psychologist and you feel like a child?" What's the matter with you?"

"I feel like *your* child," said Sophie. "And you're telling me you're graduating into the golden years."

"Silver is more like it," said Roma.

Sophie laughed and said, "Well, congratulations to you both."

Hugging first Roma, then Bill, she said, "I hope you got a place with a guestroom."

"Two," said Bill.

"Can I have the one with the ocean view?"

"What ocean view? We're about four miles inland, right on the ninth fairway. You want to see water, there's a nice pond with a fountain in the middle. Don't go too close, though. I understand there are alligators on the golf course."

"Those aren't alligators," said Sophie, "they're little old caddies who've been out in the sun too long."

"Very funny," said Bill, laughing. "My daughter's a comedian."

Bill stroked Sophie's hair and said, "Why are we standing here in the foyer? Let's go upstairs. Take off your coats and make yourself comfortable."

"Who bought *this* house?" asked Sophie as they walked up to the living room.

"An Indian family," said Bill. "There are lots of Indians here now."

"What's left of my belongings? Have you given my fuzzy dog to my niece, too? You know —the black-and-white one I got from Aunt Lenore?"

Sophie couldn't believe she'd never named him.

"No, we dumped him out years ago. His stuffing was falling on the carpet."

Sophie felt a stab of regret for not having removed her crib mate when she moved to Boston. Her parents didn't share her sentimentality.

"Out!" Roma bellowed suddenly, making Sophie and Bob jump. "If something is useless to us, out it goes. OUT!"

"Jesus, Ma, you just scared the hell out of me," said Sophie, swinging around to face Roma.

The sapphire and diamond necklace flapped against her collarbone. Roma grabbed the necklace and pulled Sophie toward her for a closer look.

"What's this?" She said. "Bill, look at this."

"It's a birthday gift from Bobby's mother. Look, it comes with matching earrings."

Sophie cocked her head and swept her hair away from her earlobes.

"That's some birthday present," said Bill, looking at the necklace from beneath his eyeglasses. "We were going to give you a fifty-dollar check."

"This is a family heirloom," said Sophie. "It belonged to Bobby's great-grandmother."

Roma had fallen strangely silent. She stood biting a lip.

"What's the matter, Mom?" asked Bob.

Bob didn't miss much.

"Go sit on the couch," Roma said. "I have to get something from inside. Bill, you stay here with the kids."

"Ma, is everything okay?" Sophie asked.

Roma was already halfway down the hall. She waved a hand behind her and said, "Go sit. I'll be right in."

Sophie, Bob and Bill settled into the living room, which remained unchanged from Sophie's childhood. Sophie wondered when the blond Kranich and Bach piano had last been tuned. She reached for a handful of Raisinets on the marble coffee table. "What's with Mom?" she asked Bill.

"I guess we'll soon find out."

Roma walked into the living room carrying a small carton. She pulled out a thick glass saltshaker with a dented tin lid and said, "Remember this?"

"Of course, I do," said Sophie. "That's Gram's kosher saltshaker."

"Actually, it's your Nana Sofia's kosher saltshaker. It's old as the hills."

"I would imagine," said Sophie, hefting its weight.

"Would you like it?"

"Yes, very much. Does it still have its original salt?"

Roma gave her a look and put the saltshaker aside. She removed a round metal music box from the carton. She lifted the box's tattered lid and it slowly croaked out *White Christmas.*

Sophie took the box from her mother's hands and stroked its smooth surface. Turning it upside down, she twisted a key and the music came out faster. Sophie closed her eyes and her memory drifted to her grandmother's bedroom in the Bronx.

"This is the music box that Gram kept on her dresser," she said. "It sat on a mirrored tray, surrounded by perfumes and porcelain figurines."

The open music box let off a scent of facial powder, old metal and a hint of garlic. "I want this box," she said.

"You got it," said Roma. "Your grandmother wanted you to have it. Now, here comes the piece de resistance."

Roma withdrew a cardboard box from the carton and held it up with a tongue in her cheek.

"Why are you talking in French and making a face?" asked Sophie.

"This is something I didn't expect to give you today."

"I see you're still hesitating," said Sophie.

"Under the circumstances, I don't think I should wait," said Roma. "Take it quick before I change my mind."

Sophie snatched the box out of her mother's cold hand and said, "What's the big mystery?" She looked at Bob and said, "I'm almost afraid to open it." To her father she asked, "Do you know what's inside?"

"No," said Bill. "I've never seen that box before. Your mother is full of surprises. Go ahead and open it. I'm very curious to see what she's been hiding from me all these years."

Sophie held the box on her lap and took a deep breath before removing the lid. A piece of batting covered the contents. Sophie peeled the thick cotton off and gazed at an exquisite sapphire and diamond ring in an old-fashioned setting. She removed the ring and placed it on her finger. The platinum warmed quickly against her skin.

"It fits like Cinderella's glass slipper," she said.

"That doesn't surprise me," said Roma. "The day before Nana Sofia died, she told me that I would have a daughter and that this daughter would be the rightful owner of this ring. I was going to wait to give it to you until you had a daughter of your own, but when I saw that the ring matched the necklace and earrings you're wearing, I knew I had to give it to you now. Happy birthday."

Overcome, Sophie blurted, "Do I still get my fifty-dollar check?"

21

Sophie and Bob perched on their knees in front of the hope chest in the Gordon's musty basement. A lone uncovered bulb hung from the ceiling, casting off a weak circle of light.

"How can I part with any of this stuff?" asked Sophie, sifting through the treasures of her youth. "How can I throw out my two baby dolls or my Golden Books? I learned how to read with *Puppy and Me*. Look, the kid in the book looks just like me." She lifted the book to show Bob, who squinted at the page.

"Take it all," said Bob. "You can even take the two baby outfits. You'd look adorable in that blue sundress right now."

Bob kissed her on the cheek.

Sophie waved him away. "Look, here's an old diary from my teenage years. Better yet, don't look."

Sophie continued to dig.

At the bottom of the chest, Sophie's eyes fell upon a child's crayon drawing of a young woman. A piece of brittle tape still adhered to the top of the paper and Sophie needed to peel it up gently. Holding the picture before her, she said, "I recognize this person." The next minute, she was holding her chest. "I'm having trouble breathing," she said, struggling to rise but lacking the strength.

"Lie down," said Bob. "There are decades of mold in this basement. I can hardly breathe myself."

Bob put Sophie's head in his lap and stroked her hair. Sophie closed her eyes and tried to calm down. Where had she seen that face before?

Bob took the drawing from Sophie's hand and held it up to take a closer look. A chill prickled his neck and the picture swam before his eyes, forcing him to turn away.

"Did you draw this?" he asked.

Sophie opened her eyes before responding and saw a picture of a dark-haired man gazing down at her. She gasped, "I know him."

She snatched the paper out of Bob's hand.

"Who is he?" asked Bob.

"I don't know."

A deep blush made its way down Sophie's face and chest, penetrating deeply and filling her with embarrassed pleasure. She could almost feel the man's bones and sinew and flesh against her body. If his lips could move, she felt certain they would speak her name. Why couldn't she remember who he was? Maybe her parents would know.

Bob still sat looking at the picture of the woman, a puzzled furrow between his brows. Where had he seen this woman before? Maybe she resembled one of his old aunts. Bob squeezed his eyes shut against the sharp and sudden memory of wiping tears from the woman's velvety cheekbones with splayed thumbs. He fought an impulse to crumple the picture and bury it deep in the ground.

Sophie squeezed Bob's leg and said, "I don't remember drawing these pictures, but that doesn't mean I didn't." She sat up abruptly and tossed the paper into the pile of keepers in the box. "I have all I need from my past," she said. "Let's close the chest and get the hell out of this clammy basement."

Bob stood and helped her up with one gentle tug of his wiry arms. He bent to lift the box of salvaged possessions.

"Do we need to bring the drawings?" he asked. "They're giving me the creeps."

"I want to ask my folks about them," said Sophie, nonchalantly, taking the pictures from the top of the pile. She wouldn't admit how enthralled she was by the man's portrait and how comforted by the woman's.

Bill and Roma were in the kitchen finishing their lunch. Bill was lifting matzo shards with a damp finger and depositing them in his mouth. Roma was licking the remnants of her low-fat cottage cheese off a tablespoon. Three prune pits lay in a saucer beside her bowl.

"Who wants to share my Granny Smith?" asked Bill when Sophie and Bob entered the kitchen with their box.

"They don't want apples now," said Roma. "They haven't had lunch yet. What can I do you for?"

"What have you got?" asked Sophie, leading Bob to the table.

"Bagel with Swiss cheese. Bananas with sour cream. Matzo and farmer cheese."

"Anything else? Like tuna on whole wheat?"

"I hate that tuna your mother gets," said Bill. "It tastes just like cat food."

"Maybe it *is* cat food," said Sophie. "Bob, can you eat anything?"

"Have you got any butter or cream cheese?" asked Bob.

"No," said Roma. "Why don't you have a little Swiss cheese on a bagel with mustard?"

"Is the Swiss cheese real or lo-cal?" asked Sophie.

Roma pulled the cheese from the refrigerator. "One-percent fat," she read, pointing at the words on the package with a crooked index finger.

"Tastes like plastic," mumbled Bill with a mouth full of apple.

"Sure, that'll be great, Mom. Do you have any plain bagels for Bob? You know, the ones he can actually eat?"

"Roma flung open the freezer and said, "I've got *Everything* bagels. They've got onions, sesame seeds, poppy seeds, garlic, *everything*. They're delicious."

"Okay, that'll be one *Everything* bagel with plastic cheese for me and Bob, I'm afraid you're on your own, sweetie."

Bob looked miserably at Roma. "I think I'll have another bowl of raisin bran with a banana."

"We don't have anymore milk," said Roma.

"Then, I'll have what Sophie's having."

"You'll see, it's delicious," said Roma, bustling toward the toaster oven. Her eyes lit upon the box on the floor. "What are you taking?" she asked.

"The family silver," said Sophie, pouring seltzer into a stray glass on the table.

Roma bent over, preparing to sift through the carton. She picked up the paper that sat on top. "Oh, boy," she said. "Where did you find this?"

"At the bottom of the hope chest," said Sophie. "We were hoping you could tell us about it."

"I thought that got thrown away," said Bill, shifting in his seat.

Roma said, "Of course it didn't get thrown away. Jeanette gave it to me just before she died. Remember, she kept it on her refrigerator for years."

"Did I draw that?" asked Sophie.

"Yes, when you were a little girl," said Roma.

"I guess I used to have artistic talent."

"As far as I know, they were the only drawings you ever did, outside of your coloring books. We thought the pictures were fantastic, but they upset your father."

"Who are the pictures of?" asked Bob.

He didn't want to appear too anxious, but he was dying to know.

"Sophie, do you remember Jeanette's mother, Lila? The old lady who used to live downstairs from us in Flushing, who used to take care of you?"

Sophie could see Lila's face in her mind; the kind eyes, the sagging skin, the long, unkempt hair cascading down the back of her worn cardigan.

"Of course, I remember Lila. I loved Lila. She always took me so seriously. I distinctly remember that."

"You drew those pictures the day she died. Grandma Ida thought the picture looked like Lila when she was young. Jeanette looked high and low for pictures of her mother as a girl, but couldn't find a single one. That's why your father got so upset."

"I thought you were bewitched," said Bill, with a toothpick wiggling in his mouth.

"Yeah, not to mention bothered and bewildered," added Roma.

She gave Bill a look for interrupting and went on. "Jeanette thought it was a picture of herself as a girl, but she didn't look all that much like her mother. It had to be Lila. It never made any sense, but life went on, and we forgot about it."

Bob began to relax. The woman in the picture was just an old family friend, someone who had taken care of Sophie as a baby. Maybe the picture just showed how a little child would see an older person. Maybe he had tender feelings toward this woman because she had nurtured the woman he loved. Still, there was something so familiar about the pale eyes and the set of the mouth.

"What about the guy on the back?" Sophie asked.

"Zayde, as a young man," said Bill.

"Zayde? Did I know Zayde?"

"Zayde died shortly after you were born," said Roma. "He was a quiet man. I barely knew him. But, Grandma recognized her father. His name was Gershon."

Sophie's head jolted up at the sound of her great-grandfather's name.

"What sort of a man was he?" she asked, settling her eyes back down on the picture.

"I only knew my grandfather as an old man," said Roma. "His hands shook when he gave us peppermints. I think he gave your Nana Sofia plenty of trouble when he was younger. There was a big secret between them. But, they stayed together all the years. She was a strong woman, Nana."

Roma clattered two plates in front of Sophie and Bob and said, "Eat." Bob obediently bit into a bagel, chewing slowly.

"Aren't you going to put something on that?" asked Sophie.

"Why should I?" asked Bob. "It's already got *everything*." He swallowed with a grimace.

"Suit yourself," said Sophie, reaching for the mustard with a knife in her hand. Bob took one look at the blade and pushed himself back from the table with a screech of chair legs against the linoleum floor. His plate sailed off the table like a flying saucer and landed with a crash.

"What is it?" shouted the family in unison. As Bob bolted out of his chair, Sophie could see the whites of his eyes above and below his irises. "Bob, what's wrong?" she shouted. "Is it a roach?"

Bob hated insects. He didn't seem to hear her.

Bob turned on a heel and hurtled down the stairs to the front door and fled from the house. He ran down the tree-lined street without stopping to look over his shoulder. He ran for his life, on wet pavement, dodging children playing touch football. Moisture collected in his hair and fogged his glasses. He ran until he forgot why he was running and stopped abruptly, winded, bending at the waist with his hands on his thighs.

Sophie met him halfway back to the house. She held his jacket out and helped him into it.

"Let's finish lunch and head home," she said.

She would save her questions for later when they were far away from *Everything* bagels and the gaze of ancient faces.

Massachusetts 1985

22

Bob lay sound asleep in the passenger seat of Sophie's car. They were already north of Bridgeport. As Sophie passed the turn-off for her favorite rest stop, she throbbed with a few involuntary pelvic contractions. As she sighed behind the wheel, she remembered where she had last encountered the man who looked like her great-grandfather, Gershon. It was on the day she learned her grandmother had cancer. A stranger at the hospital had given her a menthol cigarette. Then, he disappeared off the face of the earth. How long had it taken for him to fade from her thoughts?

Sophie saw Bob stir and she took his hand in hers.

"Are you feeling better, sweetie?" she asked.

"That was some visit," he mumbled. "I don't even remember getting into your car."

"You gave us all a scare, taking off like that," said Sophie. "My mother thought you had snapped at the prospect of eating plastic cheese. I told her that you probably didn't have a plastic cheese phobia bad enough to send you running for your life."

Sophie started to laugh, but Bob's lifeless expression stopped her mid-ha.

"It was the knife," he said.

"What knife?"

"You were reaching for the Gulden's with a knife. To me, it looked like a butcher knife aimed at my throat."

"It was a butter knife, Bobby. If my parents actually kept butter in their house, I could've slathered you with it, but I don't think it would have been a fatal smearing."

Bob looked at her and said, "It does sound pretty crazy, doesn't it?"

Sophie kept her eyes on the road and said, "I don't know. We both reacted pretty strongly to those pictures. Maybe they stirred some kind of memory for us."

"I could understand why they would stir memories for you but why would they affect me?"

"Good question." Sophie looked at Bob and gave him a weak smile.

"Are the drawings in the box?"

"Yes, I decided to keep them. They're such bizarre artifacts. I couldn't just toss them out."

"I wonder what your great-grandparents' big secret was. Think there was a skeleton in their closet?"

"I'm more concerned about there being a skeleton in *our* closet."

"I have no secrets, Sophie. Do you?"

Bob looked at her out of the corner of his eye.

Sophie squirmed in her seat as she felt another unexpected contraction seize her groin. She swept beads of sudden sweat off her forehead. Sophie swerved onto the exit ramp and headed west, into the country.

"What are you doing? That wasn't our exit. Where are you going?"

Sophie ignored Bob's questions and drove in silence until the lights of the highway faded away. She pulled into the gravel parking lot of a deserted fruit stand and stopped the car. She turned to look at Bob who was staring at her with raised eyebrows.

"Get into the back seat," said Sophie.

"What is this, a stick-up? Am I being kidnapped? What the hell is going on, Sophie?"

Sophie bent forward and kissed Bob hard on the mouth. Backing up to look him in the eyes, she said, "It's either the back seat or the weeds, baby."

"It's raining out," Bob protested.

"Then, it's either the back seat or the wet weeds. You pick."

"I pick we wait until we get home to our nice, dry bed."

"Okay, then, you don't get to pick. Get into the back seat."

Bob didn't budge. Sophie got out of the car and walked around to the passenger side. She started to undress slowly and deliberately, her body ethereal in the mist. Bob leaped out of the car and threw his arms around her. He looked around for perverts lurking in the bushes.

"What's gotten into you?" he hissed. "Get into the car before someone comes down the road and sees you."

Sophie broke away and danced in circles with her arms and face upraised. Bob's exasperated look transformed into a leer. He picked her up mid-spin and carefully slid her rain-slicked body across the back seat of the car.

Unzipping his jeans, Bob opened Sophie's legs and entered her while she laced her ankles against the small of his back. Sophie lifted her bottom to maximize Bob's penetration while he pressed his shins against the doorframe for traction. "

Sofia, you're killing me," Bob moaned as he came and collapsed between Sophie's cold breasts.

Sophie caressed her husband's damp hair and frowned up at the ceiling.

"Bobby, did you just call me Sofia?"

Bob raised his head and looked down at his wife in the dark car. A streetlamp had come on and he could clearly see the raindrops on the rear window. The upper half of Sophie's face was in a shadow. Her hair hung down like a shroud, straight and pale. Something was wrong with the lower half of her face. Didn't Sophie's chin come to a point? Why did her chin look squared and cleft? Bob reared back and let out a terrified scream. The mouth was Lila's mouth, the woman in the drawing. Bob scrambled out of the car, tripping on the weeds, struggling into his pants.

He could hear the woman shouting from the car, "Max, where are you going in such a hurry?"

For the second time that day, Bob found himself sprinting away from the woman he loved in a state of confused panic. Discomfort and fatigue sharpened his sense of reason and he slowed his pace.

"Fucking *Everything* bagel probably contained psilocybin," he muttered to himself between ragged breaths. He bent over the trash-strewn grass and shook the rain from his hair like a dog.

"Bobby! Where the hell are you?" shouted Sophie.

Bob could see her silhouetted against the light of the streetlamp and the voice was unmistakably Sophie's. He straightened and walked toward her, hoping he wouldn't have to run off again. He wanted to get home to his warm, dry house and put this day behind him.

"I'm getting too old for this shit," he said as he approached Sophie.

"You've got to stop running off on me, Bobby. I'm sorry I took the wrong exit, but that's no reason for you to leave me alone on the side of the road."

Bob noticed that Sophie was fully dressed and that her curly hair was dry. Her hands were cold and trembling. He cupped them in his warm palms and blew on the slender fingertips.

"Why did you take off like that?" asked Sophie.

Bob hesitated to answer. Had he merely imagined the events of the past twenty minutes?

"Why do you think?" he ventured.

"I think you need to drive for a while," said Sophie. "You've been acting crazy ever since you saw those pictures this morning. I'm exhausted. You take over and get me home. And, I'd better not wake up in the Bronx or some damn place."

Bob lifted Sophie's chin and kissed her lightly on the lips. They were Sophie's lips, full and red. He opened the passenger door and helped her in. As he walked around the car to get to the driver's side, he noticed that the back door was ajar. He felt a twinge of returning fright, but stood his ground.

"Sophie," he called through the car, "Do you have everything you need from the back?"

Sophie didn't answer. She had already dozed off. Bob nodded and said, "All right, then."

He closed the back door with a flip of his hip and slid into the driver's seat. He was going straight home, no matter what. He was relieved to see his gas tank was more than half-full.

23

Bob carved the apple carefully, cutting it first in half, then in quarters. With quick flicks of his wrist, he excised its tough, seedy core. He put a segment in his mouth and savored its tart, astringent taste. As Bob chewed, he tried to focus on the brief in front of him. Sophie had gone out to shop. Bob would have the house to himself for a couple of hours. He looked at the kitchen clock and blew all the air out of his lungs. It was a few minutes before one in the afternoon. He checked his watch for a second opinion and resumed staring at his brief. He put another piece of apple in his mouth.

Bob's roiling mind transferred to the box in the garage. He had left it beside a stack of oilcans. Maybe he should go down there and bring it upstairs. Sophie hadn't mentioned it this morning. She'd only remarked on how heavily she'd slept. Bob had had to carry her up to bed the night before. They hadn't discussed the seduction at the fruit stand, nor had they spoken of Bob's frenzied flight into the weeds. Bob would make it a point to speak with Sophie when she returned from the store.

Bob's case notes blurred before his eyes and he reached for another piece of apple. He put it in his mouth and Lila's face invaded his thoughts. She'd called him Max. Bob began to choke and spat the apple out. "Jesus," he muttered. He got up from the table and threw the upchucked apple into the garbage disposal.

Bob scooped water into his hands at the kitchen sink and splashed his face. As he toweled off, he turned to face the door leading down to the garage. He folded the towel over the back of a kitchen chair and reached for the doorknob. His hand hovered as if reluctant to commit to a grasp.

What was he afraid of in his own home? Cursing himself, he abruptly twisted the knob and hurled the door open. He grimaced when he heard the door crash against the doorstop. "Okay, then," he said as he trotted down the stairs and entered the garage. Bob spotted the box and approached it with a clattering heart. He checked his watch again. He didn't want Sophie to catch him sneaking a visit with her drawings. He had to work quickly.

Bob bent to retrieve the piece of paper that had been on the top of the pile the night before. It wasn't there. Where did it go? Bob's upper lip beaded with sweat as he rummaged through the box. He removed every item and swept his hand across the bottom. Nothing. He settled back on his haunches. Could the damned thing have blown away? No, he had seen it before he went up to bed the night before. Maybe Sophie took it when she left earlier. Bob's eyes welled up with tears. He needed to see those pictures.

Bob carefully placed Sophie's possessions back in the box and straightened with creaking joints. He kicked the box back next to the oilcans and trudged up the stairs. He looked around the kitchen. The room was just as he left it, but the light had changed. Bob checked the wall clock again. One eleven. Why was the room so dark? Bob approached the kitchen table and saw that his last apple wedge had turned to rust. A bright half moon was visible through the bay window.

Where had the last twelve hours gone? When had day become night? He had been in the basement for minutes, not hours. Was he losing his mind?

Bob's chest contracted with a sharp intake of breath, exhaling with a panicked shout, "Sophie?"

Where was his wife at this hour? Bob charged up the dark stairs, his knees buckling on every step. The bedroom door was open. "What?" Sophie cried. She was sitting straight up in the bed, with the sheet pulled taught across her breasts. "Why are you yelling like that? You scared me! What are you doing up?"

Bob sat on the edge of the bed, and shook his head. "I'm the one who's scared. Who are you?"

Sophie turned and clicked on the end-table lamp. She pulled the sheet up to her throat and waited for her husband to continue.

Bob looked intently at Sophie. Beneath the sleep-tossed curls, the left side of her face was fully illuminated. Bob extended his hand and turned the rest of her face toward the pale gold light.

"Don't blind me," said Sophie, shutting her eyes against the full impact of the lamp. She struggled against his grip, but he held her fast. "What are you looking for?" she shouted. A trace of panic put a tremor in a voice.

"Where did you put those pictures we brought home?" Bob demanded.

"On my dresser. What's gotten into you?"

"When did you put them there?"

"This morning. I got up early. You were dead to the world. I went outside to bring in the newspaper and suddenly, I was afraid we'd left my belongings in New York. I went looking for the box and there it was, in the garage. I opened it and took the pictures out. I figured they'd been buried long enough. I'm surprised you didn't see them when you woke up."

Bob released Sophie's chin and got up from the bed. He walked over to Sophie's dresser and picked up the drawings.

"What did you do today?" Bob asked.

He held the picture of Lila so he could see her in the moonlight. Her eyes peered into his. Bob felt like she was reading his thoughts.

"I went shopping and got home around four. You were working at the kitchen table. I didn't want to disturb you. I unpacked the groceries and went up to the den to work on a crossword. I also reviewed a couple of patient files for tomorrow. Of course, I'm going to be exhausted tomorrow because you're keeping me up with the third degree all night. And, you were screaming, Bobby, *screaming.*"

"Did you and I speak at all today?" asked Bob nonchalantly.

"Of course, we spoke. What's the matter with you? I think you're working too hard, Bobby. Come to bed."

"Sophie, did anything unusual happen on the way home from New York?"

"Yes. I let you drive."

"No, I mean really strange. Like, did we have sex on the road?"

"In your dreams," Sophie laughed.

Bob didn't join her. He stood looking at Lila's face.

"Birnbaum," he said.

"What?"

"Was Lila's last name Birnbaum?"

"Maybe. The name does sound familiar. I believe her husband's first name was Max."

Bob felt cold.

"That's what she called me," he said.

"Who's she?"

Bob didn't answer. He kept his back to Sophie, his stance rigid.

"Put the paper down and come to bed."

Sophie's voice sounded strident in her own ears. She could hardly recognize it. She softened her tone.

"Bobby, please lie down with me. We'll throw those damned drawings out in the morning. Throw them out now, if you want. Just come to bed and hold me."

Bob turned around slowly and saw his wife extending her arms to him from their bed. The sheet had dropped, revealing the perfection of her upper body. He felt relieved to see the familiar curve of her waist. He left the pictures on the dresser and moved toward his wife and her warm embrace.

New York 1910

24

Max Birnbaum got off the boat on wobbly legs after three disorienting weeks at sea. He held his young sister's hand. Strange men pointed at his banana-yellow suit and laughed, calling him a greenhorn. He understood the insult only when the men tore his jacket up the back and pulled the scarf from Anya's braided hair.

Max spoke no English. He pushed his sister behind him to protect her from their assailants. A man in a uniform came forward and roughly shoved the thugs away, retrieving Anya's scarf. That's how Max and Anya spent their first five minutes in America.

Max didn't dwell on the mean-spirited louts on the dock. He had experienced far worse in Russia. Ignorance and cruelty was everywhere, but here, in America, one could at least hope for better. The torn jacket seam was a fleeting annoyance. Max was a master tailor, and he had brought his sewing kit on the journey. Still, it would've been nice to look presentable when his older brother, Yakov, came to retrieve him and Anya from Immigration. He took the jacket off and folded it over his arm. He turned his fair face to the warm August sun.

Yakov had come to America from Kiev three years before. He now co-owned a garment factory in lower Manhattan and was happy to employ his talented brother. In the meantime, Anya would marry Yakov's recently-widowed partner, Mischa. Mischa's children were nearly grown and he looked forward to having more with a young wife.

Anya had been sent to America with a cumbersome dowry of down-filled linens. Mischa's nephew, Gershon, was powerful enough to lift two-hundred-pound bolts of cloth, so Mischa brought him along to help with Anya's luggage. Mischa wanted to focus on his young fiancé without huffing and puffing over her belongings like a red-faced old man. He wanted to kiss her smooth cheek and present her with a sapphire and diamond necklace and matching earrings.

Anya was far more attracted to Gershon than to his uncle. Gershon was strong and handsome and closer to her own age. She soon learned that Gershon was already married. The weight of the jewels against her collarbone was some small consolation. She would be a rich man's wife. At least Gershon would be in the family.

When Max reached out to shake Gershon's hand, Gershon took him in a full embrace and whispered in Russian, "Brother, the first thing you must do in America is get rid of that yellow suit."

The two men stood laughing, rocking back and forth in each other's arms.

Max was older than Gershon, but Gershon was worldlier. Gershon had been in America longer and was already a husband and father. He had a feral allure and smelled of whiskey. Max was natty and genteel, and had never been with a woman.

Gershon had brought two women to America; his wife, Sofia, and her friend, Lila. Lila had spent her life taking care of other people's children, including Gershon's. She had tended to Sofia when she was a child. Now, Lila was well past thirty and standoffish with the men he'd brought home to meet her. She was far too prim for his Uncle Mischa.

"Who are you waiting for, the King of England?" Gershon would bellow.

"Leave me alone, Gershon," Lila would say. "I don't need any of your trashy friends pawing at me."

"You're not getting younger, Lila. Don't you want children of your own?"

"I'm too old to start in with that now."

"You're a handsome woman, Lila. You should have a family of your own."

"You and Sofia and the kids are my family."

"You need your own man, Lila."

"Find me a halfway-decent one and I'll think about it."

"I've brought home plenty of good men."

"They're a bunch of drunks and gamblers."

Gershon shook his head and looked at his wife under hooded lids.

"She's not wrong," Sofia would say.

"I'm going out," Gershon would say, and the argument would end until the next time.

When Gershon met Max, he saw a perfect man for Lila; a pure, calm man with polished manners and a good work ethic. He brought Max home for dinner one night after work and Lila blushed when Max shook her hand. When Max wasn't looking, Lila gave Gershon a sly nod and placed an extra lump of sugar in his tea.

Lila reminded Max of his gentle, efficient mother, whom he missed and would never see again. Max and Lila got married within the year and Lila conceived their one and only child, Jeanette.

For several years, Max enjoyed a life of order and habit. He awoke every morning at five-thirty. Lila got up with him to fix his tea and hand him his hat on the way out the door. He was at his sewing machine by seven. He took two cigarette breaks a day, one at ten, the other at three, always with Gershon. Rain or shine, the men went out to the alley behind the factory and smoked standing up, pressing their backs against the building's cold brick.

At eleven-thirty, Max and Gershon had sandwiches and pie at the automat on the corner. On Mondays, Wednesdays and Fridays, Max left work promptly at five and headed home to Lila and Jeanette. On Tuesdays and Thursdays, Lila kept his dinner warm on the stove while he attended meetings of the Odd Fellows. He never joined Gershon for nights of boilermakers and crap shooting.

On Tuesdays and Thursdays, Max left the Odd Fellows early and spent the rest of the evening in the shadows across the street from Gershon's apartment with his hat brim pulled down low. He stood crouched, with his hands in his pockets, hoping for a glimpse of Sofia. Sometimes, she would part a curtain and look out on the night with a cigarette held aloft between two slender fingers. The tip glowed red as she inhaled the unfiltered smoke. When the desire to go to her became too great, he turned and fled home to the family he wouldn't betray.

Sofia wouldn't be interested in him, he reasoned. She and Gershon fought like savages, but the looks they exchanged between battles locked out the rest of the world. The Birnbaums and Polokovs spent most of their Sundays together, sharing meals and playing cards in each other's parlors. On more than one occasion, Max had walked in on Gershon and Sofia enmeshed in a dark corner. Max had envied them to the point of despair.

One night, as Max drifted toward merciful sleep, Lila put her hand on his shoulder and asked, "Has Gershon been showing up for work?"

Max opened his eyes halfway and said, "Yes, dear. Why do you ask?"

"Sofia tells me he's been coming home drunk late at night with empty pockets and sob stories. Can't you say something to him?"

A moment passed before Max responded. Why had he ignored his friend's bloodshot eyes and trembling hands? Gershon couldn't even eat anymore. When they went to the automat, Gershon sat with a roll in one hand and a spoon in the other, aimlessly stirring the thin soup that never made it to his mouth. Why hadn't Max said anything?

"How long has this been going on?" he asked.

"Long enough," said Lila. "Sofia has always been too independent. She waits until there's a crisis before she speaks up. They're living on noodles over there. You've got to speak to him, Max. Tell me you will."

"I can talk to him. I can't guarantee he'll listen."

"Does Mischa know what's going on with him?"

"Gershon's been doing his share of the work. What he does with his personal life is *his* business. Besides, Mischa has his hands full with my sister and the babies. I ask you, why does a fifty-year-old man need infants to chase?"

"Don't change the subject. You and Gershon are like brothers. Do what you can to make him see reason or we're going to have to put his whole family up in our living room."

"There's barely room for us in this apartment."

"Yes, Max, I know that. That's why you don't have a minute to lose."

Max turned in bed to face his wife. He looked at her pale, frowning countenance in the moonlight and said, "I will speak with him tomorrow."

"Promise me."

"I promise. Can we go to sleep now?"

Lila gave him a direct stare with her colorless eyes for a full minute before saying, "Yes, my love."

She patted Max's cheek and turned away from him. Max settled down against his pillow with his hands under his head and stared at the ceiling. It was true that he and Gershon were like brothers, but it was Sofia that he loved. He imagined the taste of her full lips and his legs writhed against the chilly sheets.

25

In the nightmare moments before waking, Max dreaded the mission ahead of him. He had made a promise to his wife that on this day he would speak to his best friend about changing his ways. Max struggled with what approach he would take. The bottom line would be, "Do it for Sofia." Max wanted to do it for Sofia. He began to toss in his sleep. Someone began caressing his hair with long fingers whispering, "Bobby, wake up. You're having a bad dream."

Bob tossed his head from side to side like a spooked horse and clung to sleep. In his dream, he saw Max kissing his wife good-bye that morning. Lila had handed him his hat, just like always. He went to work, intending to speak with Gershon during lunch and get it over with. He would say, "You have responsibilities to Sofia and the children. Tell me what you owe the sharks and we will work things out."

Surely, Gershon would come to his senses.

When Max went to the back alley for his first smoke, he saw Gershon squatting sullenly against a wall, staring vacantly ahead. He looked ill, his cheeks sunken. The skin beneath his eyes was a smoky blue.

"Gershon," Max yelled from a respectful distance, "how about a little pinochle this weekend?"

Gershon didn't appear to hear him. He hunkered down and withdrew a bone-handled knife from his coat pocket. Unsheathing it, he began to scrape it against a flat stone that lay in the dust at his feet. Max heard the rasp across the alley. He reluctantly approached his friend. The dank air smelled of rotten produce.

Max attempted a joke. "What are you doing, Gershon? You prefer mumblety-peg? That we can play right now. Only I left *my* knife at home."

Gershon looked up at Max with tears in his eyes and placed the blade of the knife against one sinewy wrist. "It's no good, Max. No good."

Max froze in his place. He was afraid that a step in any direction would result in disaster.

"Nothing is so terrible it can't be fixed, Gershon. I'll help you. You sure helped me enough. I wouldn't have made it here without you, for God's sake. Put the knife down and get up. You're just having a bad spell."

Gershon continued to look at him, the tears flowing freely down his lean cheeks, the knife still poised.

"Help me by looking after Sofia and my daughters. I've let them all down."

Max jabbed his fingernails into his palms to keep from enjoying the possibility of taking care of Sofia.

"Don't be a fool, Gershon. Sofia and the girls need *you*, not me. You just need to get a hold of yourself. If you need money, get it from your uncle. I'll help you pay him back. How much are you into the shylocks for?"

"Too much. I'll never get out from under. My family will be better off in your hands. I love Sofia that much."

"Your family belongs in *your* hands, not mine. You're drunk and a little out of your head, but that doesn't have to be true tomorrow."

Max thrust his hand forward and said, "Give me that knife."

Gershon looked down at the knife and appeared to be considering his options. The knife glinted against the fish-underbelly pallor of his skin. Max saw the ripple of Gershon's thick blue veins rising up for the blade.

"That's not the way," Max said, realizing too late the wrongness of his words.

Gershon withdrew the knife from his wrist and abruptly slashed his neck. "Forgive me," he gasped as a line of dark blood rushed to the surface.

"Stop it," screamed Max, lurching forward and landing on his friend. Gershon didn't try to get out of the way. He held up his hands to break Max's fall and the sharpened knife, its edge already stained with Gershon's blood, accidentally plunged into the base of Max's throat. Max never uttered a sound. He fell spread-eagled on top of Gershon, his long coat blanketing the two of them. Warm blood bathed Gershon's face until he could no longer see the still horrified look in Max's eyes.

As their blood mingled and spread beneath the warm cocoon of Max's coat, Gershon felt safe for the first time in years. Instead of screaming in anguish, Gershon closed his eyes and happily dozed as if he were in his mother's featherbed. All his troubles seemed to dissolve beneath Max's body.

Massachusetts 1985

26

From a distance, Bob heard Sophie's panicked voice. "Wake up, Bobby. Wake up now." He felt a pounding in his chest. Sophie was pummeling him with all her might, and still he did not wake up.

Bob's mind returned to the alley, where the bodies of Max and Gershon lay in a heap. A co-worker's screams roused Gershon back to consciousness. He woke with sober horror, covered in blood that had cooled and congealed.

"I'm alive," he whispered.

The co-worker didn't hear him. He screamed and screamed in the gory alley until others came.

"I'm not dead," he shouted, over and over.

"Bobby, wake up," Sophie shouted.

She was shaking him now. She was pinching his nose and breathing into his mouth.

"Don't die on me, for God's sake."

In Bob's dream, Gershon whispered, "We had an accident. I am not dead."

As he lay unheard amid the hysteria, Gershon knew that he would go on living. He would find a way to pay his debts. He would take care of his family. He would take care of Lila and Jeanette. Gershon held Max beneath the sheltering coat and wept.

Bob woke up with tears in his eyes and Sophie's breath in his lungs. He began to cough. Sophie reared back and cried, "You stopped breathing, Bobby. I couldn't wake you up and all of a sudden, you weren't breathing at all. I think you're sick from those goddamn drawings and we're going to get rid of them. Now."

"I'm not dead," said Bob, wearily.

"No, you're definitely undead. Don't even say it. Come downstairs with me."

Bob took her arm before she could rise.

"I had the worst dream," he said. "Only, it didn't seem like a dream. It felt real, like I was living in a different body. I saw myself differently. My thoughts were another man's thoughts. It was horrible. I saw myself dead, Sophie. One minute, I was fighting with Gershon. The next minute, I was dead. Yet, I continued to experience the whole thing through Gershon's eyes. It was so real, Sophie. Please, throw those drawings out. Get rid of them. Burn them. They're driving me out of my mind."

Sophie stroked Bob's clammy forehead and said, "It feels like you have a fever that's breaking. Maybe you'll feel better now." She kissed his parched lips and said, "We'll destroy the pictures now. We don't need them in this house."

Sophie peeled the comforter back and gasped. The sheet beneath them was stained with fresh blood.

Bob jumped and shouted, "What is it?"

Sophie forced calmness into her voice. "It's nothing, Bobby. My period started, that's all. Stay under the covers until I get back. I'll change the sheets later."

Sophie wadded up a handful of tissues from the bedside table and placed it between her legs. Waddling off to the bathroom with her hands holding the tissues in place, she passed the picture of Gershon on the dresser. He appeared to watch her with his pale eyes. Sophie felt a surge of heat in her groin. When she removed the tissues, she expelled a clear, viscous liquid, untainted by blood. Sophie did not attempt to wash the wetness away. She placed a hand against the base of her stomach and felt an unfamiliar fullness. She wrapped herself in a towel and returned to the bedroom. Bob was no longer in bed and the pictures were gone.

Sophie found Bob rummaging through the kitchen junk drawer for a lighter. He shoved aside rubber bands, batteries and birthday candles before landing on a prehistoric Bic. Bob held the drawings over the kitchen sink and flicked the lighter. The Bic produced a weak blaze that browned the edge of the paper. Bob watched the flames licking at the side of Lila's square jaw. When he noticed Sophie in the kitchen, he quickly blew the fire out. Sparks spiraled up toward the ceiling and disappeared.

"You don't have to stop," said Sophie. "We don't need the drawings to remember them."

Bob sat heavily on a kitchen chair and laid the charred paper down on the table. Why couldn't he burn the damned thing? Something in Lila's eyes beseeched him to stop. He felt an overwhelming sadness when he looked at her. He turned her picture over and his sadness turned to terror. Looking at Gershon felt like a glimpse in his own mirror. Bob pushed the picture away, but couldn't escape shreds of memory.

"I knew him," gasped Bob. "I knew Lila. I knew Sofia. I knew them all."

"I knew them, too," said Sophie quietly with her head down.

Bob's breathing calmed down as he looked at this wife. "Well, of course you knew them, or knew about them. They were part of your family."

"More than that."

"How much more, Sophie? Did you know that Gershon killed Lila's husband?"

"Yes, Bobby, I knew that."

"You knew? Why didn't you tell me before?"

I didn't realize it until just moments ago."

"What didn't you realize? What's going on here?"

"It was *you* Gershon killed, Bobby. "*You* were Max Birnbaum. Lila was your wife."

Bob stared at Sophie across the table. "But that's preposterous. Isn't it?"

Sophie put her hand on Bob's. "I'm going to tell you something and I want you to keep your mind open. I remember you as Max. You were a dear man and a very good friend to Gershon. I'm sure you intended to help him. He loved you very much. He wanted to be more like you. After you died, he actually succeeded in becoming more like you. It was as if the two of you had merged. In the end, you managed to save us all."

Bob sat stiffly in his chair and asked, "How do you know all this?"

"Because I was Sofia."

Bob abruptly rose from the table, crumpled the drawings and hurled them into the trashcan beneath the kitchen sink.

"I've had enough of this," he said, without looking at her. "I'm going to work."

Massachusetts 1987

27

Sophie slowly swayed back and forth in her rocking chair and held the baby close. The little girl sucked on two long, delicate fingers as she slept, making chirping sounds like a young bird.

"She's the image of your grandmother," said Roma for the hundredth time.

"Her name is just perfect for her, then, isn't it?" said Sophie.

"Grandma would be very happy that you named the baby for her," said Roma.

"Who else would I name her for?" Sophie stroked her daughter's downy hair and cooed, "How could I have lived so long without my little Idina?"

'She's delicious," said Bill.

"Perhaps you can have her later with a side of yams," said Sophie.

"And lima beans," said Bill. "You don't want to forget about the lima beans."

"Certainly not," said Sophie, smiling at her father.

"It's going to be hard for you with Bob gone," said Bill. "Do you want to move down to Florida? That way, we could be of help."

"There's no reason to uproot myself. My life is here. I have at least forty years to go before I move to Boca."

"Who's going to take care of things while you're working?" asked Bill.

"I'll hire a nanny. That's what people do now."

"Back when you and Ron were small, Grandma and Grandpa were a big help," said Roma. "They practically raised you."

"Unfortunately, things aren't like that anymore. Hey—why don't you move to Boston?"

"Are you crazy?" shrieked Roma. "We're going to leave Paradise to shovel snow? No, thanks."

"Mother's poker cronies couldn't live without her," said Bill.

"Well, all right, then. It's settled. We'll do just fine all by ourselves." Sophie kissed the sleeping baby's head. Idina continued sucking contentedly. Sophie was all she needed.

"The insurance money should help," said Bill.

Sophie looked up and said, "Yes, it's a shame Bob had to die for me to get it."

Bill could never tell when his daughter was being facetious. After living with Roma for forty years, murderous eyes just looked like myopia to him.

"It's a terrible shame that such a young man should die like that," said Roma. "He never even got to see his own daughter. It's not going to be so easy for you to find another man."

"Thanks, Ma. I'll keep that in mind when I put myself back on the market."

Sophie didn't bother to mention that another man had already stepped up to the plate. Roma and Bill would be appalled. Better to keep Patrick a secret for now.

A nurse stepped into the room and asked Sophie, "Are you ready to go home?"

"I'm not sure. You've taken such good care of us, Millie."

"You'll do fine on your own. How are you feeling?"

"Like a milk truck. Aside from that, never better." Sophie smiled and added, "Tell you the truth, Millie, nothing has ever felt this good."

Millie looked at Roma and Bill and asked, "Are you the grandparents?"

"Does it show?" asked Bill.

"Idina's the image of my mother," Roma said.

"Your mother must have been absolutely gorgeous, then," said Millie. "Idina's one of the prettiest babies I've ever seen. She sure loves her mommy."

"And, I sure love her," said Sophie, slipping Idina's silky strands of hair through her fingers.

Bill said, "It's a shame her father couldn't see her."

Millie looked at Sophie with her brow furrowed and saw Sophie shaking her head. Millie had met Patrick, but apparently, Sophie's parents had not. She played along.

"He would've been so proud," she said. "Sophie, I'm going to bring your discharge papers and an orderly with a wheelchair. It's time to throw you all out of here."

Millie smiled and left the room.

Bill asked, "What can we do?"

"Why don't you take my suitcase and baby paraphernalia to the car? We'll probably be wheeled to the main entrance in a few minutes."

"I need a cig," Roma said, mostly to herself.

"Better do it now, Ma. I don't want the baby to be around smoke, certainly not in the car."

"All right, all right. I'll be right back."

Roma scooted out of the room, the pack of Newports already in her hand. Bill proceeded to pick up everything in the room.

"Dad," said Sophie, "Our bags are already packed and in the closet, ready to go. There's no need to gather thermometers and bedpans and sugar packets."

Bill, put his booty down sighing and ambled over to the closet.

"Ach," he said, "such excitement."

"Yes, it's been a wild year. I'm really glad that you and Mom made it up here."

"My daughter should give birth and I shouldn't come?" asked Bill. "Of course, I'm here. Where else would I be now?"

"In Paradise playing shuffleboard?"

"Not this week. Some things are more important."

Bill squeezed his daughter's shoulder.

"Bet you had to crowbar Mom out of the clubhouse."

"What are you, kidding? We're happy to be here for you, honey. Don't be so hard on your mother. She loves you."

Sophie nodded vacantly and said, "Dad, before Mom gets back, tell me, did you know Zayde personally?"

"Yes, but he died shortly after you were born. Why do you ask?"

"What was he like?"

Bill considered for a moment and said, "I was only fifteen when I first met him. You know, your mother and I were kids when we met. He treated us like kids. He gave us peppermints. He showed us card tricks. He amazed us with his strength by cracking walnuts with his hands. He hardly ever left your great-grandmother's side. Whenever she was cooking, he was right there in the kitchen, sitting in his chair, drinking his glass of tea. Sometimes, he would walk up behind her and give her a hug. Your mother and I used to get embarrassed when we caught them in the act. He was crazy about your great-grandmother. And, you were the apple of his eye. What more can I tell you?"

"How did he die?"

"His heart failed," said Bill.

Sophie turned away to keep Bill from seeing the abrupt welling of tears in her eyes. Millie came into the room with an orderly. She carried a small blue bundle in her arms.

"Guess who got sprung from his incubator?"

Sophie's eyes grew wide, "What a surprise. Can I take him now?"

"You sure can. He's as healthy as can be."

Tears ran freely down Sophie's checks as she reached out an arm for her son.

Bill rushed to Sophie's side and said, "Why are you crying?"

"New mother hormones," said Millie, smiling. "You and the twins are going to be just fine, Sophie—better than fine. Are you ready to go?"

Sophie nodded and asked, "How are we going to do this?"

Just then, Roma reappeared, reeking of smoke and with a wild look in her eyes.

"You okay, Ma? You look like you saw a ghost."

"I just had the scariest experience in the lounge. There were only a couple of people in there. I sat down on a couch to relax a little. I looked out the window for a minute and all of a sudden, I saw a reflection of a man who looked just like my grandfather as a young man in the glass. I turned around, half expecting him to not be there, but there he was, just sitting in a chair with his hands together. I don't remember seeing him there when I walked in. I guess I was staring at him because he looked back and gave me a big smile. Boy, was he good looking, and he wasn't wearing a wedding ring, Sophie. Anyway, I asked him if his wife just had a baby and he just nodded. I congratulated him and told him that he looked very familiar. He told me he got that a lot. I walked out of that room with my hair standing up."

"Wow, that is strange," said Sophie.

Inwardly, she was very pleased that Roma thought that Patrick was so handsome. Sophie wondered when the two of them would meet again. Roma's hair would never be the same again when she learned that Patrick was Idina and Max's father.

Millie took charge. "Okay, it's time for all you healthy people to leave. Sophie, let your parents take the babies while I help you into the wheelchair. After you're settled, you may hold both babies as I wheel you to the front entrance. Your parents can carry your belongings out to your car and drive it around to the main entrance. We'll play it by ear from there. First, sign these papers. They're your ticket to ride."

"What a production. What am I going to do tomorrow?"

"You'll manage," Millie said.

Sophie scratched her signature on the discharge papers and handed them back to the nurse. Millie hoisted her from the rocker and settled her in a wheel chair. Both babies were placed in Sophie's arms. The baby weight was already mostly gone. She'd be back to size four in a week, but her breasts would look like balloons for a year.

As Sophie's entourage proceeded down the hall, Patrick watched from the waiting room. He considered the pink and blue bundles he saw protruding from Sophie's arms as she was pushed along the corridor. He had expected the girl. The boy was a surprise to him, as he had been to them all. Sophie had insisted on calling the boy Max. Patrick had seen him before Sophie had, clinging to life in the infant's intensive care unit. Max was a survivor, a fighter. Patrick would have to bear that in mind as his son grew to manhood and pray that Max would not be cursed with the gift of memory.

Massachusetts 1986

28

The night before Sophie met Patrick, she saw him in her dreams. Ida and Gabe were walking in a long procession through a landscape of lush meadows and rolling hills. Sophie watched them approach from far away. When they arrived at Sophie's watching place, she broke into the line to embrace them. "I've missed you so much," she cried.

Ida said, "It is not time for you to join this procession, beloved Sophie. You may join us for a short distance, but no more."

"But, it's been so long since I've seen you," Sophie protested.

"You will find us again someday. The line continually moves forward, but kindred souls always meet again. You've been allowed on the line to receive a message."

"What is it, Gram?"

"A man will come to see you. His name will be Patrick McKay. He was once my father, Gershon."

"Your father was an Irishman?" Sophie asked.

"He is now," said Ida with a grin that pleated her cheeks like an accordion.

Sobering, she said, "Listen to the message now. Patrick McKay's been waiting for the right time to come to you. You have seen him many times before, but he's been elusive. The next time you see him, he will not leave."

"Is he an angel, Gram?"

Ida laughed and said, "Far from it, sweetheart. He's just our destiny."

"Are you happy, Gram?"

"Yes, I'm very happy, sweetheart, because I know I'm returning to you. The next time you see me, you will be cradling me in your arms and my skin will be smooth and pink. Watch for Patrick McKay."

"But, what about my husband?"

"I'm sorry, Sophie. Bob will soon be joining the procession, but don't despair. He is also destined to return to you."

"Why hasn't Grandpa spoken? Why could I feel you but not him?"

"Grandpa has already been reborn."

Ida pulled Sophie forward and kissed her gently on the lips. She whispered, "I have delivered my message and now you must get off the line, sweetheart. Wake up now and answer the door."

Sophie's eyes fluttered open and she turned her head to look at the bedside clock. It was ten in the morning and she wondered why the alarm hadn't gone off. She would have to race to get to her eleven o'clock appointment. She felt so relaxed, she considered calling her patient and canceling. It felt good to laze in bed with the late-morning sun warming the room. She had slept so deeply, she didn't recall dreaming. Had Bob even attempted to wake her?

Sophie threw back the covers and headed toward the shower. As she lathered her hair, she thought she heard the doorbell ring. Probably a Jehovah's Witness thought Sophie as she worked the foam. Who else was going to show up unannounced at that hour? Girl Scouts? Telegram? Flowers? Land shark? Sophie giggled in the steamy stall and decided she would treat herself to brunch after her appointment. Maybe she would call Bob at his office and see if he had time to join her. They spoke more over brunch than over any other meal.

Sophie dressed quickly and put her coat on in the foyer. Before she turned to go to the garage, she noticed a yellow piece of paper affixed to the outside of the glass entry. Sophie opened the front door and snatched the paper off the glass. Fed-Ex had a package for Bob. They would call again tomorrow if someone had not come by after four this afternoon to pick it up. Sophie made a mental note to mention it to Bob when she spoke with him later that day.

Sophie arrived at her office on Commonwealth Avenue moments before her patient. Sophie thought of Marilyn as her autopilot patient.

Marilyn had been coming every other week for two years. She was a high school gym teacher who came to vent. She made it clear from the beginning that she was not seeking advice, just a sympathetic ear. Sophie settled into her leather chair with a pad in her lap and prepared to listen to Marilyn's latest litany for the next fifty minutes. Her stomach was already growling. She fought the urge to look at her watch. She listened to the ululations of sirens and wondered what real tragedy was taking place as she sat scratching notes and drawing hangman doodles.

A few moments before noon, Sophie called Bob at his office. His secretary told her that he was meeting with a client off-site and would not be available until early afternoon. Sophie hung up and made a beeline for the nearest Magic Pan, where she gorged on apple crepes and black coffee. She had had a craving for baked apples since waking. Her Grandma Ida used to make the most wonderful baked apples, served with a light topping of cinnamon and sweet cream. The crepes were a poor substitute, but they still satisfied Sophie's hunger.

Sophie's workload was light that afternoon. She decided to shop on Newbury Street. It was a bright winter day with a brisk wind that brought color to her cheeks. Sophie was bubbling with a peculiar enthusiasm. She hadn't felt this energetic in a long time.

Late in the day, Sophie called Bob's office again and was told he was still out. "Is he still with the same client?" she asked.

"No," responded the secretary. "Frankly, I don't know where he is."

"It's such a great day, maybe he's doing the same thing I'm doing—loafing," joked Sophie.

The secretary joked back saying, "Yeah, what am *I* doing here? Am I the only person working in Boston today?"

Sophie thanked the secretary and checked her watch. It was past four. She walked to the parking lot with her coat collar raised to protect her face from a wind that had abruptly strengthened with the approach of twilight. Sophie threw her packages into her car and slid into the driver's seat, huffing from the cold. She had one more stop. She would pick up Bob's package at the Fed-Ex office and have it waiting for him when he got home.

The line was short. A broad-shouldered man in a long gray coat and navy stocking cap was in front of her at the counter, filling out paperwork. The attendant was applying tape to his shipping carton. The tape dispenser went around and around with a raucous caw. Sophie rocked on the balls of her feet. In her boot heels, she came up to the man's shoulder.

The man handed his completed shipping form to the attendant after she removed his carton from the scale.

"That'll be thirty-two dollars, Mr. McKay," said the attendant. "How would you like to pay for that?"

Sophie stopped bouncing at the sound of his name. A warm sliver of anticipation slipped into her chest. Sophie hugged her arms and focused on the wooly fabric of the man's coat. Grandpa Gabe used to have a coat like that, she thought.

McKay reached a broad hand into his coat pocket and pulled out a weathered wallet.

"Cash," he said in a deep, hoarse voice.

He placed the bills on the countertop and the attendant presented him with his receipt.

"Thank you, Mr. McKay. Have a good evening. Next in line, please."

Sophie stepped forward as McKay turned from the counter. Her face warmed as their eyes met. She had seen his face countless times before, but he passed her without saying a word.

Sophie stepped up to the counter and said, "I believe you have a package for Max Birnbaum?"

Sophie turned and saw McKay's back stiffen before he went out the glass door.

"Actually, scratch that. I'm picking up a package for Bob Stern."

The attendant asked Sophie to wait while she searched for the package in a back room. Sophie grew impatient and kept eyeing the door. The two people in the line behind her were getting infected with her agitation. They began to fidget with their packages. If the attendant didn't show up with Bob's package in the next ten seconds, she was going to have to bolt out of the room. She needed to find McKay, even if she made a fool of herself.

"Come on, come on," muttered Sophie.

The attendant returned to the counter and asked Sophie to sign for the package. Sophie scrawled her signature and ran, jostling the person behind her.

"Sorry," she called over her shoulder as she fled.

Sophie stood in the street, looking to the left and right. McKay was gone. Deflated, she shuffled back to her car with Bob's package under her arm.

As she inserted her car key into the lock, she heard someone walk up behind her. She spun around and bumped directly into McKay's chest. The package dropped to the ground.

"Don't be scared," he said before she could call out. "You are where you need to be."

McKay bent and picked up the package and said, "This isn't for your husband. It's for me."

29

The two stood facing each other without touching. Sophie took a long look at McKay and said, "I know you."

McKay said nothing. Sophie took a step forward and McKay caught her in his arms. They clung tightly together and then sprung explosively apart. Sophie stood unsteadily, not knowing if she would spring forward again or flee.

"What's going on here?" Sophie demanded. "Do you know?"

"Yes," said McKay.

"Why did you take my husband's package?"

McKay held the padded envelope out to her, keeping his distance.

Sophie took the package and saw that it was made out to Bob Stern. The sender was Patrick McKay, the man who stood before her.

"It would appear that you are the sender of this package, Mr. McKay, not the recipient. What's going on? Who are you? What is your relationship to my husband?"

"What's in the package will explain a lot, Sophie. You said that you know me. You do. And, Bob and I go back a long, long way."

Sophie stumbled back against her car asked, "How do you know my name?"

McKay didn't move. He said, "Please open the package."

"It's made out to Bob, not me."

"Bob will understand. Open it."

Sophie shifted her purse onto her shoulder and held the package in both hands. She pulled the cardboard tab from left to right and looked at McKay before sliding a hand into the envelope. She extracted a smaller envelope containing three photographs. She held them up and said, "I can't see these. It's too dark out here."

"There's a coffee shop on Newbury Street. Come with me and we'll look at them together."

Sophie clasped the package to her chest and said, "I'll look at them at home with my husband."

McKay put a hand on Sophie's arm. He said, "Look at them now with me. Bob will understand."

"Why do you keep saying Bob will understand? What's there to understand?"

Sophie found herself leaning into McKay again, the mysterious package pressed between them. Even in the dark, his eyes penetrated her. Her breathing sounded ragged in her ears.

"Don't be afraid of me," said McKay. "This day has been a long time in coming."

"I don't know what you're talking about."

Sophie heard the words come from her mouth, but she was having trouble believing them. She knew this man. She knew his touch. She knew his smell. She knew what it felt like to love and hate him, all at once. She asked, "How did you get to be Patrick?"

"It's only a name, Sophie."

"Are you married?"

"I was married. It didn't take."

"Any children?"

"Not yet."

Sophie began to shiver.

"You're getting cold," said McKay. "Let's get something hot into you."

He pulled her hair back and kissed her hard and deep, bracing her neck with his hand. Sophie was too overcome to resist. She couldn't get close fast enough. She even forgave the silly line. She fumbled with his buttons and thrust her hands inside his coat, searching for an opening that would lead to bare skin. Her chills thawed to beads of sweat.

"Do you live nearby?" she asked.

"I live a few blocks down, on Marlborough."

"Let's go there. We can take my car."

"Leave the car here. Just come."

McKay took Sophie by the hand and half-dragged her the short distance to his apartment. Sophie was going to get home very late that night. Bob crossed her mind and disappeared. She would have her work cut out for her tomorrow, but tonight, she felt compelled to be with this stranger. Bob would have to understand.

30

The pictures were forgotten. When McKay shut the door to his apartment, he and Sophie were enshrouded in darkness. McKay kept it that way. He wrapped an arm around Sophie's waist and propelled her backward, guiding her, kissing her. If there were any obstacles in their path, Sophie didn't know about them and didn't care about them. She knew McKay wouldn't let her fall until he was ready to lie down with her, or maybe they would just push back forever. Neither of them made a sound and the apartment was silent.

They did not leave a trail of clothing in a parody of passion. The kiss itself went on and on and Sophie was happy to keep her eyes shut and fully taste McKay's mouth. When they finally exhausted the apartment's full length, they stood against a wall and slowly undressed each other.

Sophie whispered, "I want to see you."

McKay said, "Feel me first" and gently lay her on his bed. He pushed himself inside of her and all Sophie could think about was McKay's welcome weight sinking into her bones.

They fell into short dozes and woke with limbs entwined, mouth breathing into mouth, eyes connecting briefly before closing back into sleep. Sometime in the night, Sophie woke fully and realized that the room was growing light. She was going to have to go home and face Bob.

"Patrick," she whispered.

McKay rolled over on his back and pulled her on top of him. Her breasts flattened against his hard chest. She opened her legs and straddled his body. As Sophie moved her hips, she looked down at McKay in the near-dawn light and saw a man she had always known and, yet, he was a stranger, too. Sophie stopped moving.

McKay gently squeezed her hips and asked, "What's the matter?"

"I need to see those pictures."

McKay laughed and said, "Now?"

Sophie smiled back and said, "Maybe in a few minutes."

McKay pulled himself up into a sitting position and wrapped her legs around his lower back. They rocked until they surged into some shared space far above McKay's deep blue sheets and fell back into a doze. The phone woke them. It was five-thirty in the morning.

McKay grabbed the receiver and said, "Yes?" When nobody responded, he said, "Hello? Who is this?"

Sophie propped herself up on an elbow and looked at McKay. When he hung up, she asked, "Wrong number?"

"I don't know. The caller didn't speak up."

Sophie was suddenly panicked.

"Do you think it was Bob? Do you think he tracked me down?"

"No, I most definitely do not think it was Bob."

McKay sounded annoyed. He flung his legs over the side of the bed and pulled on his pants.

"Let's go look at some pictures," he said. "Then, we can talk about Bob."

"I would like to wash up first," said Sophie.

Patrick turned on a bedside lamp and bent to kiss her. "There are clean towels in the bathroom. Take your time. I'll be in the living room when you come out."

"You're assuming I know where the living room is. You kept me in the dark last night."

"It's a new day," said Patrick. "Time to come into the light."

31

When Sophie emerged from the bathroom wrapped in a towel, she found McKay in his living room. He sat on a distressed-leather couch with his bare feet up on a wrought-iron coffee table. A standing lamp lit his face and upper body. He was wearing a Patriots tee shirt and last night's jeans.

Sophie slid next to him on the couch. The towel rode up on her thighs and she pulled it down. What did she really know about this man?

"Sports fan?" she asked.

"Former athlete."

"I was wondering how you got the broken nose."

"Running for a pass."

Sophie smiled. She felt a little like a homecoming queen. She snuggled up to McKay and said, "I guess it's time for me to see the pictures."

"Get close to the light," said McKay.

He slipped an arm around her waist and pulled her tightly beside him. He handed her the envelope.

Sophie took the package and said, "I'm a little afraid to look inside."

McKay squeezed her shoulder and said, "You came here to look inside. You already know what's inside. You just need confirmation."

Sophie extracted the packet of pictures from the envelope and held the first up to the light. The sepia print was faded but the faces were fully recognizable, as were the surroundings. It was taken shortly before Gershon left for America in the Chayevsky's parlor. The faces were clearly those of Sofia and Gershon Polokov, but they were also clearly those of Sophie Gordon Stern and Patrick McKay. Sophie stiffened but her face was impassive. She looked at the next picture.

Sofia was standing with Lila on a pier, holding an infant in her arms.

Sophie asked, "Who's the baby?"

"That's your grandmother."

Sophie said, "My God, why have I never seen this picture?"

McKay didn't respond. Sophie flipped to the last picture and clenched her teeth.

A professional photographer had taken the photo in his studio. The picture still bore the photographer's name in the lower right-hand corner. Lila and Max Birnbaum posed rigidly, staring solemnly at the camera. Sophie ran a thumb across Max's face.

"It's Bobby," she said. "How the hell can this be happening? What is this, some kind of joke?"

She turned and looked at McKay. "Where did you get these?" she asked.

"I found them in my parents' attic in Dorchester."

"That doesn't make any sense. Why would your parents have pictures of Russian immigrants in their attic?"

"The pictures have been in the attic far longer than my parents have been in the house. They're not even aware of their existence."

"I still don't get it."

Sophie's head was starting to throb. She pushed her thumbs between her brows.

"Let me try to explain."

"Please."

McKay settled into his seat and placed a hand on Sophie's thigh. He said, "I feel strongly about what I'm about to tell you. I hope you don't take it as self-serving bullshit."

"I'm not here to judge you, Patrick. Just tell me how you feel."

McKay sighed deeply and said, "I believe we're destined to go through every lifetime with the same group of people. The relationships may be different, but the people are the same. It's like an eternal partnership of conjoined souls. Have you ever passed a person on the street and experienced an immediate sense of recognition, a certain familiarity?"

Sophie nodded.

"More often than not, you move on and forget about it. Not all the people you go through your lives with bear the same weight. Most people have absolutely no recall of past lives, which is actually a good thing. It allows them to fully experience the one life they're living at the moment. They think they're starting out with a clean slate. They actually aren't, but there's no need for them to know that. It's a blessing, really."

Sophie asked, "Have we been cursed?"

McKay laughed and said, "It may sometimes feel that way. You and I have always had a very deep connection. Every time we pass out of each life, we promise to find each other in the next. We invariably do, but sometimes it takes a long time. Timing is everything. I've been watching you all your life and you've been aware of me. Physically, you preceded me into this life."

Sophie opened her eyes wide and gasped. "Have I seduced a minor?"

McKay laughed again and said, "Not even close, but you do have about ten years on me."

"You're way too young for me, Patrick."

"Get used to it. I'm it for you. And, I'm younger than you in every lifetime."

"Are you ever anything other than my husband?"

"Well, no. Like most people, we start out as strangers. We may come and go out of each other's lives. But, inevitably, we end up married. For better or for worse."

Sophie sighed and said, "I wonder which it'll be this time."

"It doesn't much matter. We still seek each other out in every lifetime. And, we unconsciously seek out others in our circle."

"Aside from you and me and Bob, who else is in our circle?"

"Aren't you wondering what became of Lila?"

"Well, yes. The last time I saw Lila, she died. I remember that distinctly and I was only three at the time."

"Do you recall what you were doing before she died?"

Sophie stared at McKay and said, "I was drawing a picture of you."

Sophie tried to rise from the couch but McKay held her gently in place. He said, "Tell me more."

"Who are you, really?"

"I am Patrick McKay and you have nothing to be afraid of. You have a few more things to tell me. I'm here to listen. Then, I will tell you about Lila."

Sophie settled back down and said, "Bob and I unearthed that drawing from a chest in my parents' basement just a couple of days ago. A young Gershon was on one side of the paper and a young Lila was on the other. Bob freaked out when he saw it and then, all hell broke loose."

Sophie tried to rise again. "I really need to get home to Bob. Something's gone terribly wrong with him. I just know it."

"Don't worry about Bob." McKay held Sophie firmly against him. Sophie made a half-hearted attempt to pull away, then settled back down.

"I *am* worried about him. I think he's in danger."

"Bob is not in danger. Stay a little while longer. Let me tell you about Lila."

Sophie leaned back against the leather cushion and said, "Will you let me go when you're finished?"

"If you want to go, I won't try to stop you."

Sophie wondered if she was dreaming. It was all so surreal. Maybe she would wake up and she and Bob would laugh about it. What harm could a dream do?

"Tell me," she said. She fixed her gaze on McKay's face.

"Lila took care of Sofia as a child and sheltered Gershon when he fled from the Tsar's army. When you were a little girl, she watched over you."

"I was with Lila every day. She was very dear to me."

"Yes, Lila was a born caretaker. She married Max late in life. She was quite a bit older than Max, but they did produce a daughter, Jeanette."

"I knew Jeanette, too. My grandmother used to look after her."

"Lila was very happy to have a child of her own, but she was particularly devoted to Ida. She actually delivered Ida, and she saved Sofia's life doing it."

"I didn't know that."

"Sofia was still weak from losing her first child. She would've lost your grandmother, too, if Lila weren't around to attend to her. Ida was a healthy baby, but Sofia had lost a lot of blood during her delivery. It took months to nurse her back to health. So, Sofia and Lila tended to Ida together and they both developed a deep attachment to your grandmother."

"I'm surprised Lila didn't get married earlier and have a whole passel of children."

"She had bigger fish to fry, in the grand scheme of things. Gershon brought Sofia and Lila and Ida to America and he introduced Lila to Max. What you don't know is that Gershon was with you on the day Lila died."

"I don't know what you're talking about. My great-grandfather died soon after I was born."

"You haven't been paying attention to what I've been saying. Gershon was there—just not in the flesh yet. How else do you think three-year-old Sophie was able to draw a picture of him as a young man?"

Sophie reared back and said, "Are you telling me the picture was alive?"

"In a manner of speaking, yes. The picture was a conduit; a portal into the next life, if you will."

Sophie shook her head, and said, "What was Gershon doing there?"

"He was there to remind you of who you were and to plant a seed of recognition that would germinate as you grew to adulthood. He wanted you to feel safe when he presented himself to you again."

"What about Lila?"

"He needed her for what was to come next."

"Which was?"

"To give birth to Patrick H. McKay."

"Jesus Horatio Christ."

Actually, the H in my name stands for Henry."

Sophie smirked and said, "So, you're Patrick Henry?"

"Yes."

"Well, give me liberty or give me death."

McKay laughed and said, "Turns out, there's not much difference between the two."

"I'm afraid to ask, is Lila still alive?"

"Oh, yes, very much so. And, this time around, she actually does have a passel of kids, all grown now. I have a sister named Lila. However, the Lila of your childhood, Max's Lila, has no recall of that former life. She could pass Max in the street and keep going without batting an eyelash. She's a fifty-six-year-old housewife named Meghan McKay. My father, John, owns a liquor store in Revere."

"Did you ever say anything to her about your former life?"

"Are you kidding? You can't spring something like that on the uninitiated. It's a rare gift to remember previous lives. Meghan McKay does not possess that gift. If I ever suggested she was anything other than what she was, she'd call the priest and try to organize an exorcism."

"When did you become aware of your own former lives?"

"When I was around three, same as you. My parents thought I was strange—and I certainly was—but I learned to fit in. You can't screw around with oddball stuff like that in Dorchester. I was a good student and ended up going to Boston College on a football scholarship. I even played a little pro ball for a while."

"What do you do now?"

"I'm an architect."

Sophie sniffed and said, "I'll say you are. I'm afraid of what's going to come out of your mouth next. You're not going to tell me my Grandpa Gabe came back as your pet Irish setter, are you?"

"McKay laughed and said, "No, he's still waiting in the wings for your Grandma Ida." Sobering, he said, "And, in nine months and seventeen years, his wait will be over. That's who you're carrying in your belly right now."

32

Sophie rose slowly from the couch and pulled the towel taut across her chest. "That's patently absurd," she said, staring hard at McKay.

She bent at the waist and started to collect her belongings from the floor.

"What part of this is *not* patently absurd? If I said the same thing to someone without your gift, they'd never believe me. But, you've got to believe me, Sophie. Your Grandma Ida will live again and you will give her that life."

"Stop it, Patrick, for Christ's sake. As if all of this wasn't insane enough. Now you've got me visualizing a little gray-haired parasite in bifocals busting out of me and calling me 'sweetheart'. I miss my grandmother. I would love to see her again, but not like this."

"Relax, Sophie. She may not have a memory this time around."

"Great. She won't know from nothing, but I'll be looking over her shoulder every two minutes, waiting for the day she turns her Play-Doh into matzo balls."

McKay laughed and said, "Let's not worry about that now. Just know that Ida will be reborn to the only people she can be reborn to— you and me. If she shares our gift, it'll be apparent by the time she turns three. That seems to be the age of first recognition."

"Why don't I just show her the pictures I drew at three and see if she develops a craving for borscht?"

"That wouldn't be advisable. In fact, I want you to get rid of those drawings."

Sophie retrieved her shoes from beneath a lamp table and asked, "What's the sudden rush?"

"Those drawings will only complicate things."

"For whom?"

"For everybody. Believe me. I'm not asking you to get rid of them. I'm telling you."

"All right, all right, they're already gone. Bob threw them out this morning before he left for work. Speaking of Bob, I must get home to him. He must be worried-sick. I don't know what I'm going to tell him."

McKay sat on the couch watching her with his arms wrapped across his chest. He said, "There's no need to be rushing off, Sophie. I saw your husband today."

Sophie dropped the shoe she was holding and said, "You saw Bob? Where? When? I've been trying to reach him all day."

"He was sitting in a coffee shop on Boylston Street, reading *The Globe*. It was late morning. I came in and asked him if the stool was vacant and, without looking up, he gestured for me to take it. I sat there for a while. He didn't pay any attention to me. I ordered a cup of coffee and watched him out of the corner of my eye. I asked him for the time. He pulled his cuff back to look at his watch. It was a very Max-like gesture, by the way. When he looked up to tell me it was a few minutes past eleven, our eyes met and I could see the recognition there. He looked at me for a long time and then he folded his paper, preparing to leave."

"I'm surprised he was so calm. I would've expected him to run off. He's been doing that a lot lately."

"He did run off, Sophie, but not right away. We had a little chat, first."

Sophie's arms felt suddenly chilled. She hugged them to her chest and rocked.

"You're cold," said McKay. "Let me get you a blanket."

McKay sprung from the couch before Sophie could stop him and came back with a heavy quilt. He lay Sophie back against a pillow and wrapped her up like a mummy, tucking the quilt tightly about her.

"Do you want something hot to drink?" he asked.

Sophie shook her head. She was feeling very tired.

"Please go on," she said.

"Bob was preparing to leave when I asked, "How are you, Max?"

"That was sneaky of you."

"Didn't you do the same thing to me at the Fed-Ex office? I wanted to see his reaction. I wanted to gauge the depth of his recognition. He squinted at me and said, 'You're mistaking me for someone else.' I said, 'No, I don't think so.'"

"Bob asked, 'Have we met?' and I said, 'Yes we have, old friend.' It was at that point that I took off my cap. That's when I saw the panic come into his eyes."

"What were you trying to do, scare him to death?"

"No, I certainly did not want to do that. I guess I was curious to see if he was really making the connection."

"He was clearly making the connection. You didn't need to torment him. He's been having a hell of a week."

McKay ignored her reprimand and continued. "Bob asked, 'What do you want from me?' I said, 'Just a few minutes of your time.' He seemed amenable to that. He even settled himself back on his stool and looked at me square in the face. He glanced at his watch again and said, 'I don't have much time.'

"I asked him if he knew who I was. He said he did not, but that I reminded him of someone he knew a long time ago. I asked him if that person's name was Gershon and he said, 'Yes. Are you one of his great-grandchildren?' I said, 'Not exactly.'

'Then, who are you?' he asked.

"I told him I was an old friend of Max Birnbaum's. That got him going. He was agitated. Bob doesn't have the same sensitivity as we do, but he has some. It's been strengthening lately. I think that, on some level, he always knew I would reappear."

"I'm sure he was really thrilled to see you," Sophie sniffed.

"Max and I used to be very close, Sophie. He died trying to save my life, you know. Did you know that he was in love with Sofia?"

Sophie pulled her arms out of the quilt and placed her hands on her ears yelling, "I don't want to hear anymore. I've heard enough. Don't tell me anymore. I'm going home."

"Don't go, Sophie. You won't find Bob there."

"Well, where the fuck is he? I don't care if you and I made a pact in another life. Bob and I have been together for more than twenty years. Our marriage is fine—at least it was fine until you showed up. Now, I'm here with you in the middle of the night, dressed in a towel and you tell me I'm pregnant with my grandmother. What kind of ungodly bullshit is this? What do you want from us, Patrick—or whoever you are?"

"I want you back."

"That's it? That's what this is all about? What if I don't want *you* back?"

"You *do* want me back. You've been waiting for me your whole life."

"And what's Bob supposed to do?"

"Bob is out of options."

Sophie disentangled herself from the blanket and threw it on the floor, but she couldn't get her legs to move.

"What are you saying to me? What the hell is that supposed to mean?"

"After Bob figured out who I was, he asked me the same question you just asked. I gave him the same answer. He shouted 'Stay away from Sophie. She's with me, now. Stay out of our lives.' He grabbed his coat and went bolting out of the coffee shop. He ran out so fast, he left his wallet on the counter. I ran after him to give it to him, but he sprinted right in front of a moving trolley. I tried to pull him out of the way, but all I got was his coat."

McKay's voice grew hoarse. "I gave a statement to the police. They took his wallet. I'm sure they've been trying to reach you all day."

Sophie's legs began to work again. She leaped at McKay and began hammering at him with her fists.

"Are you telling me that my husband is dead? Who the fuck are you, the Angel of Death? What do you do, show up every few decades and kill Bob in every incarnation? Maybe he should've killed *you* this time. That would have only been fair. Maybe *I* should kill you."

McKay dodged Sophie's kicks and said, "I've never killed anybody. It was an accident. Both times."

Sophie shouted, "Every time you show up, somebody dies."

When the neighbors started to pound on the walls. McKay pulled Sophie abruptly to his chest and held her there. Exhaustion took over and she clung to McKay's shoulders.

"Jesus, couldn't you have skipped a lifetime?" Sophie cried. "Bob didn't deserve to die like that. Why couldn't you just leave us in peace?"

McKay said, "I'm sorry, but I really did have to come. It was the only way for Ida to return, and she has to return, Sophie. She's got a message for you."

"Oh, for Christ's sake. Why don't you just tell me the message?'

"I don't know what it is. Only Ida knows. And she won't be telling you what it is for a long, long time."

"Maybe she's already delivered her message. Have you considered that?"

McKay looked puzzled and said, "Frankly, no. I sure haven't. What makes you ask that?"

"Because when I heard your name, it sounded pretty damned familiar."

"All I can say, then, Sophie, is have a little faith. Trust your instincts."

Sophie began to dress hurriedly with trembling hands. "It just seems to me that you've come into my life to take a life and give a life. I don't know what to do with you, but I'll tell you one thing. I won't be bound by a promise we supposedly made to each other in a different life. If what you say is true—if I've conceived a child on the same day that my husband died, then people will regard the events as coincidental. They'll say, 'Look at that—he died without knowing he had a child on the way. How sad.'"

Sophie began to cry again. She said, "If I'm pregnant, I'll have my husband's baby and nobody will be any the wiser. I do not have to marry you."

"Oh, but you will."

Sophie turned abruptly and slapped McKay hard across the face before crumbling into his arms. They stood entwined with McKay resting his chin on top of Sophie's head. He looked out the window and watched the sky lighten behind the brownstones across the street, calmly considering his next move. He was going to have to win Sophie's trust. Her love was a given, regardless of how she behaved. Tomorrow, he would return the old pictures to his parents' attic. Someday, he and Sophie would give them to their daughter.

33

Early the next morning, Sophie stepped into her house. Instead of its usual lemon scent, the house smelled vaguely of smoke. The kitchen was cold. Sophie walked into the hallway to check the thermostat, and it showed its usual seventy-two degrees. She shivered beneath her coat and pulled it more tightly around her. Perhaps she was coming down with something.

Sophie approached her answering machine as if it were a coiled snake. The message light flashed relentlessly. There were calls from various patients, one from her father and two from the police. The first call from the police had come in at around two in the afternoon, the next at four-fifteen. Both messages were terse.

"Mrs. Stern, this is the Suffolk County Police. There's been an accident involving your husband. Please call us as soon as you receive this message."

Sophie tensed as she listened as if she had been caught with her hand in the cookie jar. McKay had been telling her the truth. Bob was surely dead.

The phone rang, making Sophie jump. It was not yet seven in the morning. She snatched up the receiver and quavered, "This is Sophie Stern."

"It's Patrick."

"Patrick, for God's sake, I thought you were the police." Sophie relaxed her stance and waited for McKay to speak.

"I was just making sure you got home all right," he said. "Call the police as soon as we get off the line."

"What am I going to tell them? What excuse can I give for not calling them earlier?"

"Tell them you got home with a headache late in the day and fell into bed without checking your messages. When you got up and discovered your husband had still not come home, you called them immediately. Do it now. I'll speak with you later."

The phone went dead before Sophie had the chance to hang up. She dialed the number the police had left. A woman with a strong Boston accent said, "Suffolk County Police, please state your name clearly."

In a voice that was all business, Sophie said, "This is Sophie Stern. I just received your messages stating there's been an accident involving my husband, Bob Stern."

"Just a moment, Ma'am."

A man with a clear, deep voice got on the phone and identified himself as Lieutenant Ed Wiley.

"Mrs. Stern, I'm afraid I have bad news. I need you to come down to the station house."

Sophie gripped the receiver and asked, "Is my husband all right?"

"No, I'm afraid not."

Sophie's breath got locked in her chest and she felt like she might fall on her knees. She placed a hand on the wall for support.

"Mrs. Stern, are you there?"

Sophie found the strength to croak, "Yes."

"Stay with me, Mrs. Stern. Please try to remain calm. Is someone there with you?"

"No."

"I'm going to send a car for you. The officer will make sure you get here safely and we can talk then. How much time do you need to get ready?"

Sophie brushed the tears from her eyes and said, "A half-hour."

"Officer Kevin Dwight will pick you up. Is that all right, Mrs. Stern?"

Sophie said, "Yes," and hung up. She trudged upstairs to the bedroom to change. She had already showered at McKay's apartment. She searched her closet for soft, warm clothes that wouldn't bind. Her lips felt swollen from kissing McKay the night before. A red surge of shame colored her cheekbones.

Returning to the main floor of the house, Sophie withdrew a long woolen coat from the foyer closet and slipped it on, tying the belt securely around her waist. At a loss for what to do next, she sat with a purse on her lap in the living room and waited for the doorbell to ring. She was reminded of waiting for a prom date to show up, wondering if the corsage would damage the silk strap of her dress. She shivered beneath the coat.

Sophie broke into tears when she looked at the photos on the mantel. One had been taken the previous summer on the Cape. Bob was sitting bare-chested on a bicycle, smiling broadly, a Red Sox baseball cap turned backwards on his head. There was another shot of she and Bob taken at a friend's wedding two years before. Bob was in a tux, looking happy and elegant.

Sophie unwrapped a chocolate mint from the coffee table and placed it on her tongue. The cool sweetness that filled her mouth gave her a swift jolt of energy. She was reaching for another when a soft knock came at the door. Sophie withdrew her hand and lifted herself from the couch. Before she got to the door, she realized she wasn't wearing any shoes.

Sophie opened the door. A young officer extended his ID and introduced himself as Officer Dwight. Sophie nodded and said, "I'm barefoot."

Officer Dwight looked at her feet.

"Please come in," said Sophie. "I won't be a minute." She left the officer standing in the foyer while she ran to her bedroom for a pair of woolen socks and rubber-soled boots.

Her eyes lit on the bureau where her drawings had spent the night before Bob tossed them out. She made a mental note to remove them from the trash and bury them under the mattress when she got home. They were the last things that Bob had touched and she was hesitant to part with them, regardless of what Patrick told her to do.

Sophie returned soundlessly to the living room and told the officer, "I'm ready now."

She turned and locked the door before heading down the walk.

The first cold rays of winter sun were just coming up over the roofs across the street.

Dwight opened the passenger door and took Sophie's arm to help her into the seat. When he got into the driver's seat, he expressed his regret for her loss. His eyes reflected his sincerity. He was still young enough to feel, Sophie noted. She sat calmly with her hands in her lap. She looked out the window at muddy cars crawling through traffic, their gray-faced drivers sipping coffee and staring bleary-eyed as they sat in rush hour purgatory. The officer dispensed with the blue flashing light and siren. This was no emergency. They rode in silence.

The squad car pulled into a space in front of the station house. Dwight slipped out of his seat and moved quickly to open her door and help her out of the vehicle. She looked for judgment in the young officer's eyes. Why hadn't she called the police when her husband hadn't returned home? Where was she last night? What took her so long to call? Dwight was nothing but gentle and compassionate. For a minute, she wondered if he was going to take her by the hand.

Sophie asked, "Am I going to have to identify my husband?"

"I'm afraid so."

Sophie started weeping. She asked a question she already knew the answer to. "How did he die?"

Dwight said, "He got hit by a trolley. I doubt he ever knew what hit him."

Sophie cried harder. "How can this be happening?"

Dwight touched her shoulder and said, "It was an accident. Is there anyone you can call to be with you?"

Sophie thought it over. Bob's parents were both dead and his sisters lived out of state. Who was she going to call, her parents in Boca? Her friends? Who were they? She shook her head.

"I'll be with you," said the officer.

"Thank you."

"Let's have you speak with Lieutenant Wiley first."

"Okay."

"Would you like to get a cup of coffee on the way?"

"Is there tea?"

"Yeah, sure. Let's stop in the break room and I'll get some for you."

The officer led Sophie through a surprisingly quiet anteroom. She had never been in a police station before. She wondered where all the shackled "perps" and "skells" were. Nobody bustled. Few phones rang. Nobody was being interrogated behind a two-way mirror by some crew-cut cop in a bad suit.

There were two policemen sitting in the brightly lit break room, reading *The Globe*. They looked up but said nothing when Dwight and Sophie entered. Dwight plucked a Styrofoam cup out of a dispenser and showed Sophie where the teabags and hot water dispenser were.

"I think there's some sweetener and swizzle sticks around here somewhere," he said, rummaging through drawers.

"I don't need any," Sophie said. "Thanks."

She submerged a teabag in her cup and the water instantly turned a deep orange. She took a sip and welcomed its bitterness.

Dwight led her down a corridor and they stopped in front of a large office with dark wood furniture and pale olive walls. The nameplate on the desk said, Lt. Edward T. Wiley. A tall, slender man of about sixty with a thick mane of sandy gray hair and pale blue eyes stood when Sophie entered with Dwight. Dwight made introductions and Wiley stood to shake Sophie's hand in a firm grip.

"I'm sorry for your loss, Mrs. Stern. Please have a seat. Officer Dwight will rejoin us shortly."

Sophie sat and looked Wiley in the eyes while Dwight retreated from the office. Wiley hadn't asked yet why she hadn't called earlier. She sat quietly, volunteering nothing. She clasped her cup with both hands.

"This must've come as a terrible shock to you, Mrs. Stern."

"Yes."

"When did you notice your husband wasn't home?"

"When I came home last night—but it's not unusual for him to work late."

"Why didn't you call us last night?"

"I didn't receive your messages until this morning."

Sophie shifted in her seat.

"I came home last night with a blinding headache and went straight to bed. When I woke up, I saw that Bob's side of the bed hadn't been slept in and, when I went downstairs to see if he had fallen asleep in the living room, I saw the answering machine light flashing. That's when I called."

Wiley asked, "Had your husband been under a lot of stress lately?"

Sophie shuddered at the past tense.

"He's always under stress—that's nothing new. But, his behavior's been erratic these past few days."

"Erratic, how?"

"Delusional. One minute, he's okay. The next, he's seeing things and running from them."

Wiley made a pyramid of his hands and asked, "What kinds of things?"

"He claims he's seeing people from past lives and he's been feeling threatened by them."

Wiley cocked his head and said, "How long has that been going on?"

"Just for the past few days. It started at my parents' house last weekend. One minute we were having lunch, the next, he was running down the street."

"Did you consider having him checked out by a neurologist? Strange behavior like that can signal a brain tumor."

"I thought it was a one-time event. What was he doing before he... ran into traffic?"

She couldn't bring herself to say, "Got killed."

"He was sitting in a coffee shop on Boylston."

"Just sitting there?"

"According to eyewitnesses, he was sitting there having coffee and reading the paper. Then, just before he ran out, he was overheard yelling at a man that came to sit beside him. He was shouting at the man to stay away from you. That's when Mr. Stern grabbed his coat and left in a big hurry. He had left his wallet on the counter, so the other guy grabbed it and ran after him, presumably to give your husband his wallet back. It was too late."

"Jesus."

Sophie ran a hand through her hair.

"You should know that the man who was with your husband before the accident came in just before I had Officer Dwight pick you up."

Sophie swung her head up and said, "What? Who?"

"Do you know a Patrick McKay, Mrs. Stern?"

Sophie struggled to keep her voice steady. "Yes."

"How well do you know him?"

Sophie searched for an answer. She could say she knew him forever or didn't know him at all and neither would be a lie. On the other hand, if she hesitated to respond, she would be immediately suspected of lying. She calmed herself and said, "I know him quite well. In fact, I knew him long before Bob did."

Sophie felt emboldened by the truth.

"Were you involved with him?"

"How do you mean?" Sophie regretted her coyness. She added, "You mean sexually?"

"Yes."

"Yes, but that was before I met Bob."

"That's what Mr. McKay told us."

"What's he doing here?"

"We asked him to come in for additional questioning—just routine stuff. Would you prefer not to see him?"

Sophie didn't know whether to feel protective or vindictive. "I would be happy to see him. He's an old friend, and I could sure use one right now."

"Tell me, Mrs. Stern, were Mr. McKay and Mr. Stern rivals?"

Sophie took a minute to collect her thoughts. What was Wiley driving at? Did he suspect foul play? She answered cautiously, "I believe that Bob may have been a little jealous of Patrick. After all, I did know Patrick first."

"But you ended up with Mr. Stern."

It wasn't a question.

"Yes. Patrick and I dated when we were very young—it almost feels like it was in another lifetime. We outgrew each other, but remained close for a while. I introduced Bob to Patrick and they were quite friendly for years. They just didn't see each other very much and not at all in the past decade, as far as I know. They ran in different circles. That's why I was surprised when you said they were together yesterday. It had to be a coincidence that they met in the same coffee shop."

"That's pretty much what Mr. McKay told us."

"So, what's the problem?"

Wiley eyed Sophie over his finger pyramid and said, "There's no problem, Mrs. Stern. I'm sorry to bother you with all this. I'm sure that everything was on the up and up, but we'd like to order an autopsy anyway."

Sophie snapped, "An autopsy? Why? You want to see if he had a heart attack before the trolley hit him?"

"How did you know he got hit by a trolley?"

Sophie stammered, "Officer Dwight told me."

With a blank face, Wiley said, "I know you're very upset, but an autopsy is routine police business. We need to ascertain that Mr. Stern wasn't drugged or otherwise impaired before he went tearing off into traffic."

"Oh, for God's sake. You think that Patrick slipped him a Mickey?"

Sophie shook her head in disbelief. Why was she suddenly speaking like Edward G. Robinson?

Wiley stiffened his shoulders and Sophie said, "Pardon me, Lt. Wiley. I'm sure my husband wasn't drugged. As I said, he'd been acting strangely for days. I was keeping an eye on him. I'm a doctor myself."

"Really? What specialty?"

"I'm a psychologist."

Sophie thought she saw Wiley suppressing a smirk. She stared him down and said, "Please don't cut my husband up. I have no suspicions about Patrick—none. And, if Bob was driven to his death by some undiscovered tumor, what difference does it make now?"

"Don't you want to know what led your husband to such bizarre behavior? Was he drinking? Was he taking medications or drugs of any kind?"

Sophie said, "As far as I know, Bob was not on any meds and he rarely drank. As for drugs, do poppy seeds from *Everything* bagels count?"

"Come again?"

"Bob ate a bagel with poppy seeds at my parents house before he freaked out. Could that have affected him?"

"I doubt it," said Wiley. "But, that's why we'd like to do an autopsy."

"I don't want my husband mutilated."

Why was she being so protective of this Patrick McKay? He certainly drove Bob over whatever edge he was precariously perched on. Maybe he did slip him something. He surely slipped her something.

Wiley suddenly changed his tone and kindly asked, "Would you like Mr. McKay to accompany you to the morgue?"

Sophie searched Wiley's expression for a trick. Seeing none, she said, "Yes."

"Officer Dwight will assist you. Please let us know if there's anything else we can do."

"What about the autopsy?"

"We may just take a few samples—hair, skin, blood, like that, if you don't have any objections. Let's deal with one issue at a time. Go identify your husband first. We may be able to dispense with the full autopsy."

Sophie got up and felt like fleeing herself, before the other shoe dropped and Wiley changed his mind. Along with her grief, she had the uneasy feeling of getting away with murder. She had second thoughts about hovering over Bob's body with McKay. She half expected Bob to rise from the coroner's table and strangle them both. Maybe she would have McKay wait in another room.

Wiley dialed a number and simply said, "Mrs. Stern is ready to go. Mr. McKay will join you."

Before Dwight and McKay showed up, Wiley asked, "Mrs. Stern, is there any reason Mr. McKay would call your husband Max?"

Sophie held onto the back of a chair to steady herself.

"Max?" she said.

"Yes. When Mr. Stern ran out of the coffee shop, Mr. McKay ran after him calling him Max, according to witness reports.

Sophie said, "I have no idea. Maybe someone misunderstood him."

Wiley turned up the pressure.

"Where were you all day?" he asked.

"I was in session with a patient until noon. Afterward, I called Bob to invite him to brunch but I was told he was out. I didn't think anything of it. I ate at Magic Pan, went shopping and then went to Fed-Ex to pick up a package."

Sophie regretted the last words as soon as they left her mouth. She held her breath wondering if Wiley would inquire about the package. A slip-up like that could bring her whole house down. Sophie suddenly felt like a criminal, like she had something to cover up. Wiley let the remark go and she exhaled as slowly as she could.

"And, you went home after that?"

"No, I went back to my office. Bob told me that morning he would be home late. I had some paperwork to take care of, so I went back to my office for a couple of hours."

Sophie felt perilously close to digging a hole for herself.

"Did Bob tell you why he'd be home late?"

"No. As I said, it wasn't unusual for him to come home late. I assumed he'd be out with clients."

"What about you? Can anybody confirm your whereabouts last night?"

Sophie narrowed her eyes and asked, "Why would you need confirmation of my whereabouts? The answer is no—I was alone in my office. It was late."

"Did you run into anyone you knew while you were out and about?"

Sophie toyed with the idea of confessing that she ran into McKay, but, in reality, one could argue that he wasn't someone she actually knew—at least, not in this life. Of course, she'd already admitted they were old lovers. She wondered if anyone had noticed the scene in the parking lot or the frenzied run to McKay's apartment. She hadn't recalled seeing anyone. On the other hand, she had been so engrossed with McKay anybody else in the vicinity wouldn't have registered. She made another bold step toward deceit and waited for the ceiling to fall.

"No," she said.

The ceiling remained intact. Sophie took that as a sign to take the offensive.

"Lt. Wiley, I've just lost my husband and I'm beginning to feel like a war criminal here. Do you think I was driving the trolley that ran Bob over? Why am I being interrogated like this?"

"I'm sorry, Mrs. Stern. Let me ask just one more question and we'll be done."

Sophie stared into the lieutenant's cool eyes and braced herself.

"What time did you get home last night?"

Sophie stammered, "Around nine, I think."

All Wiley did was nod and said, "Officer Dwight and Mr. McKay have arrived."

Sophie turned and clasped McKay's hands. All she could say was, "Hello, Patrick." It was hard to believe that three hours earlier, they'd been having sex on his living room couch. His eyes looked empty, like they'd been drained for the winter. Their hands parted awkwardly and he asked, "Are you all right, Sophie?"

"I'm still in a state of shock."

"Me, too."

"We'll try to make this as painless for you both as possible," said Wiley. "Officer Dwight will accompany you to the morgue, and then see Mrs. Stern home afterward."

McKay and Sophie thanked him and turned to leave. Wiley said, "Officer Dwight, would you stay behind for a moment, please. Mrs.

Stern, Mr. McKay, please wait outside the door. Officer Dwight will be right with you." Sophie and McKay stepped out and Dwight approached the lieutenant.

"Yes sir?"

"Keep an eye on them, Officer Dwight. I think they may be hiding something. I just don't know if it had anything to do with Mr. Stern's death."

34

Bob looked like he was having a bad dream. His face was unscathed by the accident but his mouth turned downward, like he was eternally dismayed. A long, black vinyl bag concealed his body from the chin down.

"Is that your husband, Mrs. Stern?" asked Dwight.

Fighting a surge of nausea, Sophie said, "Yes," and focused on the zipper that would soon seal Bob up like an old wedding gown.

Suddenly, a small drop of blood appeared at the base of Bob's throat. Sophie called out, "He's bleeding," and wiped at the spot with her finger.

The coroner ran over and placed a hand against Bob's neck to check for a pulse. He shook his head and said, "This man is definitely dead. I see no throat wound, other than a long-healed scar."

Dwight caught Sophie as her legs buckled and half carried her out of the cold, antiseptic-smelling room. He delivered her to McKay in the waiting room, which had all the charm of a Greyhound bus station. McKay was smoking a Kool and pacing. He ground the cigarette out when Dwight came in with Sophie. He rushed over to her and said, "You're white as a sheet. I wish you let me come in there with you."

Sophie examined her finger and saw no evidence of blood there. She looked at Dwight and said, "I'm sorry about my outburst in there. Maybe my husband wasn't the only one seeing things that weren't there. I am just so tired."

"It's understandable, Mrs. Stern."

"What happened?" asked McKay.

"Nothing. I guess I was just looking for signs of life. I feel sick."

Sophie leaned against McKay and shut her eyes. He put an arm around her and pulled her close.

"When can we a make arrangements for Mr. Stern?" McKay asked Dwight, who was taking note of their intimacy.

"It depends on the results of the autopsy."

"Lt. Wiley said there might not be one," said Sophie, weakly.

"In that case, Mr. Stern's body will likely be released later today. The coroner's office will call you for instructions on where to send Mr. Stern's remains. I'm going to take you home now. Do you have someone who can stay with you?"

"If you can take me back to my car, I will follow you back to her house," said McKay. "*I* will stay with her."

Dwight looked at Sophie. Did she think McKay was being presumptuous? Apparently not—she seemed relieved to have McKay take over. He decided to ask anyhow, "Is that all right with you, Mrs. Stern?"

"Yes, I would rather not be alone right now. I have no family here and Patrick is an old friend. I'll be happy to have his help."

Dwight nodded and said, "I'm sure you're completely overwhelmed. Let's get Mr. McKay to his car and we'll both see you safely home."

Sophie said, "All right."

She disentangled herself from McKay's embrace and forced herself to align with Dwight. She walked stiffly toward the squad car and let Dwight help her into the front seat, while McKay helped himself into the back. She suddenly felt like she was dreaming, lucid but displaced. She watched the morgue fade into the background through half-closed eyes and then her eyes were shut. She heard the police radio squawking and felt the rough fabric of the seat against her cheek, but the rest of the world fell away. She focused on the vibration coming up through the floorboard as the car ventured into traffic.

At some point, the car slowed and stopped. A door slammed and then she was moving again. The car's tires made grinding noises on the sanded street. She craved lemon cake and green tea. The car stopped again and Dwight was shaking her lightly. He said, "Wake up, Mrs. Stern. You're home."

Sophie opened her eyes and saw Dwight bending toward her on

the passenger side of the car. She took his hand and said, "Thank you." Her throat was parched. She could barely recognize her own voice. Then she saw McKay standing over Dwight's dipped shoulder and her legs regained some of their strength.

"I can take it from here," said McKay.

Dwight handed Sophie off to McKay like he was the father of the bride. Dwight looked McKay in the eyes and said, "Look after her. We'll be in touch."

Sophie and McKay stood on the cement path leading to Sophie's front door and watched the officer climb into his car. It was still morning. Sophie felt dead-tired and wanted to lean on McKay but Dwight wasn't leaving. He appeared to be talking on his radio.

"Just turn and walk," McKay instructed.

Sophie plodded slowly toward her front door and dug in her purse for her key. McKay walked a couple of steps behind her, blocking her from the officer's view. He took the key from Sophie's trembling fingers and opened the door.

McKay silently took in the splendor of the high-ceilinged foyer. A marble staircase with mahogany banisters spiraled upward.

"Let's get you inside and into bed," he said.

Sophie nodded.

"When was the last time you ate something?"

"I had a mint this morning and tea at the police station."

"I'll fix you something in a minute. It'll make you feel better. Where's your bedroom?"

Sophie looked toward the stairs and slumped as she considered the insurmountable effort of climbing them.

"Hold onto the banister and take it slowly," said McKay. "I'll be right behind you if you fall."

As they trudged up the steps, Sophie said, "I think the police are onto us, Patrick."

"What's there to be onto? We didn't push Bob in front of that trolley, and they know it."

"I think they suspect we have a thing going on."

"What if they do? Adultery is not a crime. It's not savory, it might be grounds for divorce, but it's not against the law."

"God, I hate that word. Adultery. It's sounds so fucking Biblical. Like the townspeople should stone us in the public square."

"Stop talking like that. In the grand scheme of things, we didn't even commit adultery."

"Yeah, try telling that to the judge. Maybe the townspeople should stone me twice—once for adultery, once for bigamy."

"And, maybe once more for idiocy."

Sophie put on her best Bob Dylan voice and moaned, "*Everybody must get stoned.*"

She crossed the threshold into her bedroom and noticed that the bed was unmade.

"That's strange," she said, "I didn't sleep in the bed last night, but I could swear I made it before I left for work yesterday morning."

"Your mind is playing tricks on you. Do you usually make the bed?"

"I skip it occasionally."

"So, you clearly skipped it yesterday morning. Don't worry about it. Just get your clothes off and lie down. I'll go downstairs and fix you some tea and toast—if I can find the kitchen in this mansion."

"You can't miss it. It's behind the servants' quarters."

"Are you serious?"

"No. It's right next to the dining room."

Sophie had already slipped off her boots and socks and was preparing to pull off her sweater.

McKay asked, "Will you be all right on your own for a few minutes?"

"Yes. Go on down and rummage around in the fridge. Fix yourself something, too, if you're hungry."

Sophie yawned and waved McKay out of the room. After she heard him amble down the stairs, she finished undressing and put on a white flannel nightgown. She pulled down the quilt, slipped between the cold sheets and hugged Bob's pillow to her chest.

35

The aroma of rye toast and chamomile tea made Sophie feel like a child home from school with a fever. McKay appeared at the door, carrying a plate in one hand and a ceramic mug in the other. He had a cloth napkin tossed over his forearm. Sophie was propped up against her rosewood headboard, staring straight ahead.

"Somebody's been here," she said calmly.

McKay put the plate and mug down on an end table and asked, "When, since I left to fix you toast? What are you talking about?"

Sophie picked up the mug and wiped the moisture from the wood.

"I not only made this bed yesterday morning, I changed the sheets," she said. "I removed floral sheets and replaced them with white ones."

Sophie lifted Bob's pillow and said, "The last time I saw this pillowcase it was in the laundry. How did it get back on the pillow?"

"This is stress talking," said McKay. "If I go into your laundry room, I'm going to find a set of white sheets in the basket. Really, Sophie, you must eat and then you must sleep. Your mind is toying with you."

McKay sat on the bed and noted that Sophie's face looked waxy with sooty shadows forming under her eyes. She had the quilt pulled up to her chin. Her immobile legs lay straight, as if they had no joints. McKay had the uneasy feeling she was suddenly going to yank down the cover and reveal a body made of straw. He lightly touched her thigh and was relieved to feel muscle and bone beneath the blanket.

"Before you sleep, Sophie, I have to ask you something."

"What is it?"

"Didn't you tell me that Bob threw your drawings into the kitchen trash yesterday morning?"

"Yes, why?"

"The trashcan is empty. Did you empty it before you left for work?"

"I'm sure I didn't."

"Well, it didn't empty itself."

Could someone have come into my house without a search warrant?"

"Nobody official."

"How could someone have gotten in here? I keep this place locked up like Ft. Knox."

"Did you relock the door when you left with the officer this morning?"

"Yes, I'm sure I did. It's like a reflex for me."

"I don't know what to tell you. Have a bite to eat. Maybe it'll help you remember something. You've been through a lot in the past twelve hours."

The mattress squeaked as McKay rose to pick up the plate and place it on Sophie's lap. Sophie noticed he'd found the orange marmalade and applied a thin veneer to the toast. Sophie withdrew a hand from the comforter and lifted the toast to her mouth. She decided not to tell Patrick that she had intended to remove the drawings from the trash and hide them. She felt that anything that powerful should be preserved—or at least contemplated.

"Does anybody else have a key to your house?"

Sophie chewed slowly and thought it over. "My parents have a key. My next-door neighbors have a key. My maid has a key."

"It's not likely that your parents or your neighbors would come by and empty your trash. What day does your maid come?"

"Thursday."

"Wrong day. Today's Tuesday."

"Hmmm. Bob, of course, had a key. Shouldn't the police have given me his belongings?"

"I would've thought so, yes."

McKay said, "I'm wondering if someone did a little illegal research while you were out. I'm going downstairs to see if any locks have been jimmied or windows broken. It does feel cold in here."

"Patrick, why would someone go through the contents of my trashcan? The drawings weren't the only things in there. I mean, really, who would know to look in there?"

"I don't know, but I intend to find out."

McKay was on his way out of the room when Sophie said, "Can Bob still be here? I mean, I don't want to get into the whole ghost thing, but he did die violently. Isn't it possible that he's here right now, trying to communicate? You and Bob certainly had unfinished business, and not only in this life. Maybe he's here to protect me—or to harm you."

"Or to change the sheets and empty the trash?"

"Don't make fun. I'm serious. Considering these fabulous gifts of ours, isn't it just possible that relationships continue in both life and death? I feel like he's here."

McKay looked around the room and asked, "Do you see him?"

"No. But I think he sees me." Sophie began to shiver. "I'm feeling very uncomfortable with you in this room. I don't think it's right for you to be in here right now. I don't think it's safe."

"The dead can't hurt us, nor do they empty trashcans," said McKay. "Finish your toast and get some sleep. I'm going to search the house, inside and out. I'll be back up to check on you when I'm finished. Are you afraid to be up here alone?"

"No. I'm afraid for you."

"Don't be. I'm not afraid of ghosts."

"Before you go, I need to tell you something. I told the police I picked up a package at the Fed-Ex office yesterday. They didn't ask me who it was from—I guess it didn't seem relevant—but do you think they'll investigate further?"

"I doubt it. Why would they?"

"Is the package still at your apartment?"

"No. I removed the photos and threw the envelope into the incinerator shortly after you left."

"Will Fed-Ex have a record of who sent the package?"

"I guess so."

"If the police go snooping around, won't they wonder why you would Fed-Ex something to Bob if you lived in the same city—moments before you met him in a coffee shop and he went running to his death?"

McKay ran a hand through his unruly hair.

"I wish you would stop complicating matters, Sophie."

"I just want to be prepared if they put me through the third degree again. You should've seen the way Wiley was looking at me. I felt like Lizzie Borden. Did they question you, too?"

"Yes, of course. I was at the scene of the crime; remember? I was the one who reported the accident. And, no, I didn't say squat to them about running into you at the Fed-Ex office. So, stop making an issue of it."

"Humor me, Patrick. Things have gotten a little convoluted since you've come into our lives. At least, give me an alibi."

"Now, there's a criminal word for you—alibi, for Christ's sake. Okay, here's your alibi."

McKay rolled his shoulders and cracked his neck.

"If, by some miracle, the police link Bob's Fed-Ex package to me, tell them I had found some shots we had taken years ago at one of those studios that make prints look old-fashioned and decided to send them to you. I didn't want to entrust the photos to the U.S. Postal Service. They'll see we really were old friends. I'll give you the photos."

"Oh God. We're going to get the chair."

"Hey, it's the truth."

"Oh please. They may be searching your apartment right now. What if they find the damned photos there? It's not like you can give them to me right now. I'm not good at lying. If we get too creative, they're for sure going to think we killed Bob so we could be together."

"Sophie, there's no way in hell they can make us responsible for Bob's death. It was an accident. There were dozens of eyewitnesses."

"Dozens of eyewitnesses heard you call Bob Max."

"Oh, brother."

"Wiley asked me about it. I told him that you were probably

misunderstood. Should I have told them Max was Bob's nickname?"

McKay stroked his jaw and said, "I'm glad *you're* not on the police force. We really *would* get the chair."

"I'm just trying to cover all of our bases. What are you going to say if they ask?"

"If the subject comes up, I'll tell them I got flustered when Bob ran off and say the same thing you did—that the people in the coffee shop must've misunderstood me. I may have been yelling, 'Man', not 'Max'. Nobody knows who Max is anyway. It's a non-issue. Do you have any other concerns?"

Sophie sipped her tea and said, "When I saw Bob at the morgue, I wiped a spot of blood off his throat. Nobody else saw it."

"What are you talking about? The dead don't bleed. What did the coroner do?"

"He didn't see any evidence of blood—just an old scar, which I never noticed before. He certified that Bob was dead. But, I'll tell you, Patrick, when I wiped the blood spot away with my finger, it was warm to the touch."

McKay said, "That's the most unsettling thing I've heard you say."

Sophie put her cup on the carpet and said, "I can't talk anymore. All of a sudden, I can't keep my eyes open."

McKay stood and said, "I'm going to go downstairs and let you sleep for a while. Would you like me to close your door?"

Sophie nodded against her pillow, already drifting toward oblivion. As she heard McKay descending the stairs, she put a hand on Bob's pillow and whispered, "Bobby, if you're here, please forgive me."

What seemed like moments later, a gentle knock on the door had her leaping out of bed yelling, "Bobby, is that you?"

McKay opened the door and entered the room, saying, "No, it's Patrick."

He took in her white nightgown and panicked eyes and approached her as if she were a spooked horse. She took his outstretched hand and allowed herself to be led back to bed. He climbed in beside her and held her in his arms. She lay limp, but he sensed she wasn't asleep.

"Are you okay?" he asked.

He felt her nodding on his shoulder.

"Can I ask you something?"

Again, she nodded.

"When was the last time you had a fire in your fireplace?"

Sophie opened her eyes and said, "I don't know, about a month ago. Why?"

"I don't think you have to worry about anyone finding your drawings."

Sophie struggled into a sitting position and said, "What are you talking about? Did you find them?"

McKay reached into his shirt pocket and presented her with a charred shred of paper with one of Lila's eyes still visible and said, "I found what's left of them. The ashes are still warm in the grate."

Sophie took it from his hand and said, "This has got to be Bob's doing."

"Before you start getting wild thoughts about Bob rising from the dead, let me give you my theory. I think Bob may have slipped back here when you left for work, gotten the drawings out of the trash and burned them before he headed to the coffee shop. Think about it. When you called Bob's office, they said he wasn't there. They didn't know where he was. I'll bet you he was here, having a wienie roast in your living room."

"Where's the rest of the trash?"

"Where would you think?"

"Out in the big bin in the garage."

"I'd place bets that Bob hurled the rest of the trash in there. There was a fresh liner in the trashcan under the kitchen sink. He was only interested in burning the drawings, not orange rinds and chicken bones."

Sophie sagged with disappointment. She preferred to believe that her husband was still with her, but had to agree with McKay.

"That's got to be it. In fact, he tried to burn the drawings at the kitchen table this morning, but he stopped himself. I don't know why."

"Well, sometime later in the day, he changed his mind and came home to finish the job."

A sharp chill cut its way into Sophie's heart. She grabbed a hold of McKay's hair and hissed, "And then he ran into you in the flesh and died. Tell me, how did you know Bob was going to be at the coffee shop yesterday? And, how did you know I was going to the Fed-Ex office? How long have you been planning these coincidences?"

McKay pressed a thumb into Sophie's wrist and broke her grasp. He said, "I've been watching you both for a long time."

"You've been stalking us? Maybe I should call the police right now."

"I never meant any harm. You've got to believe that. I just really needed to get back together with you, Sophie. And, you really needed to get back together with me."

"Maybe you should've just invited us out to lunch and explained yourself."

"What was I supposed to say? Hey, Bob, you're married to my wife from a different life and I'm taking her back. Enjoy the baklava?"

"You could've given it a shot. Bob was a reasonable man."

"Nobody's that reasonable."

"He probably won't be that reasonable the next time you see him."

McKay frowned and said, "I don't expect to see him, Sophie."

"Oh, but you will. You of all people should know that. You will most definitely see Bob again and then things should get interesting."

McKay flung himself out of bed and said, "Do you really expect Bob to rise from the grave and come after me, rattling chains?"

"We shall see, won't we?"

Sophie was enjoying tormenting McKay just a little. For the first time that day, she smiled.

Florida 1987

36

Sophie and Patrick waited with their luggage and babies outside the baggage terminal at the West Palm Beach airport. They sat perspiring on a bench watching for a sea-foam green Mercury Marquis containing Bill and Roma Gordon. Everybody in South Florida seemed to be driving Mercury Marquis that year and the people inside of them all looked like Bill and Roma.

The noise, cigarette smoke and heat were too much for Idina and Max. They were eighteen months old and kicked to be released from their strollers. Sophie shoved bottles of tepid apple juice into their screaming mouths and fell back onto the bench beside their father.

"Why didn't your parents just park and meet us at the gate?" asked Patrick.

"They prefer to circle," said Sophie, blowing damp hair out of her face.

Patrick said, "That seems a little batty. Maybe we should've rented a car."

"Oh that would never do."

"Why not?"

"Apparently, you don't understand the politics of my people."

"Don't forget, I *am* your people."

"Then you should understand why we're waiting on a bench. Oh look, I think the people in that green car actually are my parents."

"I recognize them."

"Let's hope they don't recognize you."

The couple gathered up their belongings and made their way to the curb. The Gordon's car pulled up and Bill and Roma leaped out. Bill rushed over to Sophie and gave her a bear hug, while Roma approached

Patrick with an index finger poised to strike and one squinting eye.

"You look very familiar," she said. "Bill," she yelled over the din of traffic, "Who does he look like? It's driving me crazy."

Bill went to shake McKay's hand and looked him in the eye. "Hello Patrick. Don't mind Roma. Everybody looks familiar to her."

Roma gave Bill a look and said, "The man in the restaurant really did look like Tom Jones."

"But he wasn't."

"Of course he wasn't. What would Tom Jones be doing in our Canton House?"

"Eating moo goo gai pan?"

"Tom Jones wouldn't eat that."

Sophie struggled over to her mother, pushing two strollers, and said, "Hi, Ma." She stepped away from the carriages and the two women embraced. Roma pulled back to look at her daughter and said, "You don't look too bad. I didn't know what to expect. I was afraid you'd look all worn out from the babies and all. What's all that crap you're carrying?"

"If you're referring to my bulging backpack, you are correct. Most of what's in it is crap. Crap and apple juice."

The babies were looking up at Roma with perplexed expressions on their soft round faces.

Bill yelled, "We're going to have to get this show on the road. Traffic is backing up. Do those strollers fold up?"

Idina and Max swiveled their heads to gawk at their grandfather.

"Of course," said Sophie. "Just give us a minute to remove the babies from them first."

Patrick and Sophie lifted Idina and Max and handed one to each grandparent. With all the chaos of airport traffic, the kids were too confused to protest. Sophie and Patrick took advantage of the brief lull to fold the strollers and stuff them into Bill's oversized trunk, along with their bags.

"It's a good thing I thought to remove my golf bag," Bill said. "Which one is this?" he asked, holding a baby aloft.

"That's Max," said Sophie, shrugging out of her backpack. "We dressed him in blue so you could tell them apart."

"Looks purple in this light," said Bill, looking up and squinting. He pulled Max toward him and gave him a big kiss on the cheek. "I'm your Grandpa Bill," he said, and then added, "We're going to have to continue this conversation in the car. Somebody, quick, relieve the driver."

Sophie snatched Max away from her father and slid into the back seat of the car.

Roma asked, "Can I keep Idina with me?"

Patrick answered, "Sure. Why don't you keep Sophie company in the back seat? I'll ride up front with Mr. Gordon."

"Call me Bill. We're not formal people."

Roma said, "That sounds like a good idea. I'll sit with Sophie; you sit with Bill." She shoved Idina at Patrick and said, "Hold her for a second so I can get in. I don't want to bash her head in."

"Thanks, Ma," said Sophie.

Once Roma was seated, Patrick put Idina on her lap and said, "Hold on tight. Consider yourself a surrogate car seat."

Patrick closed the back door and slid into the front passenger seat. He tapped the dash and said, "I think we're all accounted for."

Bill said, "Hold on everybody," and screeched away from the curb, nearly nailing the traffic cop. Roma and Sophie slid across the leather seat and collided with each other, miraculously managing to keep from clunking the shrieking children together.

"Try not to kill us, Bill," Roma said.

Bill said, "Kill you? Why would I kill you?"

Roma ignored him and said, "Patrick, I'm sure I've seen you before. Bill, tell me I'm not crazy."

"Tell you the truth," Bill confessed to McKay, "you look a little like Roma's grandfather as a young man. I didn't know him when he was young, but I saw a picture once."

Roma slapped herself on the thigh, startling the hell out of Idina, and said, "That's it. Sophie, your boyfriend looks just like Zayde."

She started squinting again, struggling with a memory.

"Zayde must've been a real stud," said Sophie.

Patrick smiled at her over the back of the seat.

"Well, by the time I knew him, he was pretty old, but, yes, he was still a good-looking man. You're right, though, Bill, I'm seeing a resemblance from that old picture Sophie drew. You remember, Sophie? You and Bob took it from the hope chest when your father and I were leaving New York. There was a picture of Lila on the back—or maybe it was on the front. We could never figure out which picture you drew first."

"Let's not dwell on those drawings," said Bill. "They always gave me the creeps. How could a little girl draw such pictures? Let's drop the whole subject."

Bill maneuvered the Marquis onto Ninety Five heading south and said, "I can't wait to show you the condo. You should see the view from the kitchen. We're right on top of the golf course and there's a pond with a fountain and an alligator."

"An alligator!" said Sophie. "Do golfers ever go missing?"

"Nah, the alligator's shy. We ignore him and he ignores us. I wouldn't recommend letting the kids near him, though."

Sophie looked at her mother and asked, "Is he kidding?"

Roma looked back and said, "What do you think? Stop it, Bill. In a minute, they're going to make us take them back to the airport, and I've already defrosted the salmon."

"The children are very quiet," said Bill.

"Mine has fallen asleep," said Roma. "She's a nice little bundle."

"She was very fidgety on the plane," said Sophie. "Max did better. It was their first flight and we're all exhausted from it." Sophie kissed Max and said, "Do you want to go to sleep, too, sweetie?" Max emphatically shook his head but remained silent.

"They don't talk yet?" asked Roma.

"Oh, they talk plenty," said Sophie. "They also run around like maniacs and open cabinets and stick their heads in the toilet, so I hope you have everything under lock and key."

"How do you lock a toilet?" asked Bill.

"Just keep the bathroom door closed and the lid down, Dad."

Roma twirled one of Idina's raven curls and looked at the back of Patrick's head. "You know something? Idina has Patrick's hair."

Sophie said, "What do you mean, she has Patrick's hair? Who do I look like, the Queen of Denmark? Idina has *my* hair. So does Max."

"Your father used to have curls like that, before he lost his hair."

"Your mother likes to remind me that I'm bald."

Bill turned onto Yamato Road and blasted his horn at an aged driver who cut him off.

"Doofus!" he yelled at the closed window.

Max and Idina jumped and started screaming. Sophie and Roma soothed them with pats and clucks and Sophie said, "It's okay, Grandpa didn't mean to scare you."

Bill said, "I'm sorry. They were so quiet I forgot they were there. Tell them we're almost home. That'll calm them down."

Sophie had her doubts. She dug into her backpack and produced the remains of two bottles of apple juice.

"Are you guys thirsty?" she asked.

Both babies reached for the bottles and began sucking with their eyes opened wide.

Roma leaned forward, compressing Idina just slightly and patted Patrick's muscled shoulder, "Big guy like you must have a good appetite. Do you like salmon, Patrick?"

"Oh, yeah, I love salmon."

"What about the kids? What are they going to eat? Can they eat solid foods?"

"Sure, they just don't have very sophisticated palates," said Sophie. "I brought some food along for them to gnaw on. Wait until you see their nice little choppers. They could probably intimidate your alligator, Dad."

"Don't be so smart. This alligator is nothing to toy with. He would probably love to gobble up a couple of tasty toddlers."

Bill turned into a condo complex called Boca Breezes. He waited for a very old guard to notice his windshield decal and wave them in.

"Now the fun begins," Bill said.

Bill drove down a road lined by a hedgerow that looked like it'd been pruned an hour before with a razor blade. Bright red blooms peeked out from its dense foliage. After going the length of an Olympic swimming pool, the row of bushes abruptly stopped and revealed a lush golf course flanked by two-story condos and dotted with palms, ponds and long-legged ibises, grazing in shallow canals.

"This is beautiful, Dad," said Sophie as she gazed out the window.

"It's like the Garden of Eden with sand traps," said Patrick.

"Wait till you see the clubhouse," said Bill.

Roma squashed Idina again as she leaned over to massage Patrick's arm.

"Do you like chickpeas, Patrick?" she asked.

Patrick turned and said, "Excuse me?"

"Chickpeas. Garbanzos. You like them?"

"Yeah, sure. Do they grow wild here?"

"No, I'm putting them in your salad. I just want to make sure you like them first."

"Sure, chickpeas in the salad sound great."

Sophie shrugged at Patrick's inquisitive gaze and said, "My mother's a planner."

Bill turned onto Happy Palmetto Way and pulled into a parking space in front of a white stucco building. A coquina pathway bisected a thick lawn of St. Augustine grass, upon which sat two perfectly-trimmed palm trees dangling orange coconuts.

"We're home, kiddies," he announced. "Watch out for the anthills. Our apartment is upstairs on the right."

Patrick said, "Sophie, why don't you and your mother take the kids up? Your father and I will handle the bags. Is that okay, Bill?"

"Sure, ladies go on ahead. We'll be up in a minute. Sophie, Mother will show you to your sleeping quarters."

"Sleeping quarters? Hoo hah. Is that down the hall from the ballroom?"

"Actually, it's down the hall from the bathroom—which I promise to keep locked up like a vault.

Patrick took the backpack from Sophie's hand and said, "Let me carry that. You've toted enough today."

Sophie kissed him and said, "Please don't let my father rupture himself with the luggage. You can always make two trips. Leave the strollers in the trunk."

"Don't worry about it. Bill and I have things under control."

37

At the top of the stairs, Roma asked, "What should I do with Idina? I need to find the key."

"She can stand, Ma. Just put her down."

"She won't fall down the stairs?"

"No, just put her next to me. She's a baby, not a drunk."

With a groan, Roma transferred Idina to the ground.

"Boy, she's quite a package to carry around. I'm glad I had my kids young."

"I'm not exactly a crone, Ma."

"What are you, pushing forty? You and your brother were teenagers already by the time I was that old. Didn't you mention that Patrick was younger?"

"Yes, by ten years." Sophie's tone was defiant, but she steeled herself for what she knew would come next.

"What does he want with you; an older woman with two babies?"

Sophie put Max down beside his sister and said, "We've been through this before. Let me remind you that he came after me, not the other way around."

Truer words were never spoken.

"And, I'm a few years away from pushing forty."

"Hey, good for you," said Roma, shrugging. "You happen to make a terrific-looking couple and the kids seem very comfortable around him. You think he's after the insurance money?"

"Jesus Christ."

"All right, forget I mentioned it. He comes from good people?"

Sophie decided to lob her own grenade.

"Yes, very good. Patrick's parents have been very nice to me and they love the kids—and the kids are crazy about them. They make terrific grandparents."

Roma was still struggling with the door key, but she turned to say, "Did you and Patrick get married without telling us?"

"No."

"Then your father and I are the only grandparents your children have."

"Maybe you and the kids will get to know each other this weekend."

Roma pushed the door open and grabbed Idina and Max by the hands. "Okay, kiddies, this is where Grandma Roma and Grandpa Bill live." She pulled the children into the foyer. Idina and Max looked at Sophie over their shoulders to make sure she was following close behind. They looked liked they were dangling from twin nooses.

"Ma, please don't yank their arms out of their sockets. It's hard enough to get them dressed. And, they haven't been walking that long."

Roma dropped the children's hands and steered them into the living room by the back of their heads. Sophie followed them into the cheerful expanse of eggshell-tiled floors, a wall of windows and a combination of new and old furnishings.

"Ma, this is really nice," she said. "Look, you hung up my old gravel toreador paintings."

"Of course, I hung them up. You and your father worked on them for days."

Roma pointed the paintings out to Idina and Max and they gazed up as if the paintings were on top of Mt. Everest. A commotion at the front door announced the arrival of the men.

"We're here," sang out Bill.

"Shut the door before the mosquitoes fly in," said Roma.

"You want the bags in the guest room?" asked Bill.

"No, put them in our room. The guest room isn't big enough. I didn't realize that Patrick was a giant. Sophie and Patrick can sleep in our bed."

"We don't want to put you out of your room," Patrick protested.

"It's just for a few days, so don't worry about it. You're a big guy—you'll be more comfortable in our bed. It's a California king."

"If you're sure it wouldn't be too much trouble," said Patrick.

"No trouble. There's room in there for all of you."

Sophie stopped in her tracks and said, "You didn't get the portable cribs?"

"What do you need them for? Remember when Dad and I came for your college graduation and we all shared the bed in your apartment instead of going to a hotel? It was fine."

"It wasn't fine. It was unnatural. My roommates were ready to call the police."

"What's the difference where you sleep for a few hours?"

Sophie bit her lip and said, "I thought we had this all settled, Ma."

Bill said, "What's the problem? We were supposed to get something we didn't? I'll go get the *Yellow Pages* and find it. What are we looking for? Where's the *Yellow Pages*, Roma?"

"Mom told me you'd be getting portable cribs for Idina and Max."

"It's the first I've heard of it. Where do you get portable cribs? Do you think stores are open now?"

Sophie looked at Roma and said, "Forget it, Dad."

Patrick put an arm around Sophie's waist and said, "The kids can sleep between us, Sophie. They're little. It's just for a few days. We'll manage."

"See, Patrick doesn't have a problem," said Roma.

Roma looked at the pile of bags with her hands on her hips and said, "Boy, it looks like you're planning to stay for a month."

"Babies require a lot of paraphernalia, Ma. Speaking of which, I need to get them fed and to bed as quickly as possible or we'll all regret it later. It's been a very long day for them."

"They've been very quiet so far," said Bill.

"Enjoy it while it lasts," said Patrick. "I'm sure they'll serenade you bright and early tomorrow morning."

"I'd like to show them the Florida room first," said Roma.

Sophie didn't have the strength to argue. She looked at Patrick with a collapsed chest and drooping shoulders. Patrick lifted both children and said, "Okay, let's go see Grandma and Grandpa's Florida room.

Roma led them through the living room, with its teal-leather couches, faux-gold wall clock and plastic rubber trees and clicked a lock on a sliding glass door, tugging it open.

Sophie walked out onto the screened sun porch and said, "Wow, it's certainly Florida in here." The floor had been tiled in orange and yellow mosaics and weathered chaises were situated on either side of a small table bearing a dusty silk begonia. The late afternoon sun was going down in a blaze of golden light. They all held their hands up to protect their eyes.

"The sun is saying good night," said Patrick.

With their long eyelashes halfway down to their cheeks, Idina and Max tiredly chirped, "Night night."

"Did you hear that?" said Bill. "They said something. Did you hear that, Roma?" Roma didn't respond.

Sophie asked, "Ma, would you like to help me change the kids and get them ready for bed?"

"I think I forgot how. Do diapers still come with safety pins?"

"Cloth ones do; disposables don't. We brought disposables, and those come with tape, so you don't have to worry about stabbing them."

"I think I'll watch."

Patrick still held the children in his arms, their faces now pressed against his shoulders. "It's time for beddy-bye," he said. When Idina and Max didn't stir, he added, "I think they're already asleep. Show me where to lay them down."

Roma led the way to the master bedroom, which was dominated by an enormous shell-pink laminate bed, a matching dresser and gilded mirrors. On the dresser were several photos of Sophie and her brother Ron at various stages of development, from infantile and adorable to adolescent and hideous. Sophie picked up a bottle of Chanel Number Five, housed in a miniature golden dress pump.

"I can't believe you still have this," she said.

"What, are you kidding?" asked Roma. "I've had that bottle for at least forty years. I can't afford to use that perfume."

Bill said, "I bought that perfume for your mother in Paris in nineteen forty-four. There was a war going on. I was a soldier then."

Sophie opened the bottle with surprising ease and sniffed. Rearing back, she grimaced and said, "Pure vinegar."

"What?" Roma yelled.

Sophie smiled and said, "I'm only kidding. It still smells like Paris in the forties."

"Well, close the bottle quick before it evaporates."

Sophie put the bottle back into its shoe and asked, "Where can we put the kids so they don't fall out of bed and crack their heads open?"

Roma held out her hands and said, "Right smack in the middle of the bed. There's a mile of mattress on either side of them. We can put some pillows around them and then, when you and Patrick lay down you can take the pillows away. See, what do we need cribs for?"

"I'll go find the *Yellow Pages*," said Bill.

"Forget it, Dad. We'll manage already. Patrick and I will now demonstrate modern diaper changing techniques on your nice pink-and-white-flowered comforter."

"Put down a towel," said Roma, already racing off to the linen closet on the far side of the apartment. Sophie knew how to get her mother running like Edith Bunker.

"Forget it, Ma," Sophie called out. "We actually brought a changing sheet." Roma was already out of earshot. Sophie felt a pang of mischievous guilt.

Sophie fetched the sheet from her backpack and placed it on the front of the bed. Patrick carefully deposited both children on the cover. He and Sophie changed them and got them into sleepers without waking them. By the time Roma returned with a towel Sophie recognized from her own childhood, Idina and Max were already settled in the middle of the bed, covered with pale yellow summer-weight blankets, which Sophie had brought. Patrick placed a baby monitor on the headboard.

"What's that for?" asked Roma.

"That's so we can hear them fall out of bed all the way from the kitchen," said Sophie.

Patrick put an arm around Sophie's shoulders and said, "The kids will be fine. Relax." He looked at Roma and Bill and asked, "Would you like to kiss them good night?"

"We won't wake them?" asked Bill.

"I doubt it. They're pretty zonked out," said Patrick.

Bill looked at Sophie and she nodded for him to proceed. He crawled awkwardly from the side of the bed toward Idina and kissed her lightly on the forehead. The mattress crunched, but she didn't stir. Roma crept from the other side of the bed and hovered over Max. The little boy had two fingers in his mouth and Roma commented to Sophie, "You used to do that at his age."

As Roma bent to kiss him, Max's eyes suddenly flew open. Roma reared back and gasped, but Max remained so calm, Roma quickly recovered. She dropped her hand from her palpitating heart and patted Max's curls.

"Did I wake you, Maxie?" she asked.

Max continued to suck on his fingers but his blue eyes never left Roma's face.

Roma said, "Why is he looking at me like that? I'm breaking out in chills. It's as if he knows me."

"Well, you *are* his grandmother."

"It's more than that. You know something? He's got old man eyes."

"He's an infant, Ma. Are you telling me he's got crows feet and drooping eyelids?"

Roma gave Sophie a look and said, "I don't mean that kind of old. I mean it looks like he's been around forever—like he's seen it all already; like he knows me through and through."

Sophie crept onto the bed beside her mother and Max shifted his gaze to his mother's face. He withdrew his fingers from his mouth and gave her a toothy smile. Sophie smiled back at him.

"Hi sweetie," she said. "You like to look at Grandma?"

Max smiled and smiled.

"Go back to sleep now," she said, kissing him on the cheek. "You'll see Grandma and Grandpa in the morning."

When Sophie turned away, Max gave Roma one more sideways glance before shutting his eyes. Roma got off the bed and began rubbing her hands together vigorously.

"Okay, let me go fix dinner," she said. "You all must be starved. Are you hungry, Patrick?"

"I could eat."

The foursome walked out of the room, leaving the door open a crack. Patrick carried the receiver portion of the baby monitor toward the kitchen.

"Will we keep the kids up with that thing on?" asked Roma.

"Oh, no," said Patrick. "This is a one-way radio. We can hear them, but they can't hear us. We get to spy on them."

"That's very clever. We didn't have that kind of technology when Sophie and Ron were small."

"That's true. Ron and I were left in our cribs screaming our heads off while Mom and Dad and other assorted family members played cards in the living room. They blocked out our cries with Kate Smith and Frank Sinatra. We eventually cried ourselves into a coma."

As Bill and Roma's voices rose in protest and denial, nobody heard the light crackle of the monitor and Max murmuring, "Roma, Roma, Roma," like a mantra in his ocean of bed.

38

When Sophie and Patrick got into bed later that evening, the children hadn't budged from the dead center of the mattress. "Did you bring the monitor in from the kitchen?" Sophie asked. "I don't want my parents to overhear us."

"Yes, it's on the dresser," said Patrick. "I want to hold you."

"I want to hold you, too—but something is coming between us."

The two looked at each other over the small bodies of their sleeping children.

"How are we going to do this?" asked Sophie.

Patrick moved around the massive bed and said, "Come here."

He took Sophie by the hand and led her toward the walk-in closet. There, in the dark, surrounded by Roma's housecoats and Bill's golf sweaters, Patrick and Sophie made vertical love. When Patrick finally lowered Sophie to the carpeted floor, she whispered, "I feel really decadent, doing it in my parents' closet."

Patrick laughed. "You think you'd feel any less decadent if we did it in your parents' bed?"

"Good point. I'm wide-awake now. Can we talk for a little while before getting into the family crib?"

"Sure. Think your parents would mind if we sat in the Florida room? I don't want to wake Idina and Max."

"Not if we shut off all the lights and locked all the doors when we were through with it."

"Let's do it then."

Patrick put on running shorts and a Boston College tee shirt and Sophie threw a flowery cotton nightgown over her head. They padded through the living room with their bare feet making slapping sounds on the cool tile. Roma and Bill were in the den, watching the news. Roma was lying half-asleep on a leather recliner wearing tattered mules and a bright red muumuu. Bill was sitting bare-chested on a wrought-iron boudoir chair, flossing his teeth. He jumped up when he saw Patrick and Sophie approach, and Sophie commented on his exotic boxer shorts.

"Yellow monkeys on an orange background—where do you find stuff like that?"

"They were on sale at Burdines," said Roma, yawning.

"Shouldn't the two of you kids be asleep?" asked Bill.

Sophie noticed that Bill's chest hair had gone completely white.

"We're too wired to sleep," she said. "We would like to sit on the porch for a little while, if that's okay with you."

"Sure. Why wouldn't it be okay? Mother and I were just getting ready to lie down. Are the babies okay?"

Sleeping like logs," said Patrick.

"Come on, Roma, let's go to bed," said Bill.

Squinting and yawning, Roma said, "I can hardly hold my eyes open."

"Better get some sleep, then," Sophie said. "Tomorrow morning, when the kids wake up, we're putting them into bed with the two of you."

"Put them into bed with Mother. I get up at the crack of dawn to walk," said Bill.

"Would you like to take Idina and Max with you?"

"Let's all walk together later in the day. I'll probably be back before they're awake."

Sophie kissed her mother on the cheek and gave Bill a tight hug.

"We'll lock up before we go to bed," she said. "Have a good night. We'll see you in the morning."

"You want I should wake you up early?" asked Bill.

"No, I want you should absolutely not wake us up unless the house is on fire. The kids usually do a pretty good job of that. If all is quiet when you leave for your walk in the morning, consider it a blessing and let us sleep."

"I'll try not to wake you when I close the door."

"Thank you."

"Good night, sweetheart."

"Good night, folks," said Patrick. "Thanks again for a great dinner, Roma. The salmon was perfect."

"Glad you enjoyed it."

Roma looked Patrick up and down and said, "You've got some physique."

Sophie shook her head, but Patrick said a gracious, "Thanks," and flexed his pecs.

Patrick led Sophie through the living room to the Florida room. After opening the jalousie blinds, he unlatched the lock and slid the glass door open. As they walked onto the screened porch a sweetly-scented breeze cooled their perspiring faces. Patrick shut the door firmly behind him. They sat and looked out at the darkened golf course. They could hear the click of lawn sprinklers, the flutter of palm fronds and the croaking of bullfrogs.

"I think my mother likes you," Sophie said.

"Hey, I'm a heck of a nice guy—and a stud like your great-grandfather."

"That explains it," said Sophie, stretching out. "Odd about what happened between my mother and Max."

Patrick put his hands behind his head and leaned back with his eyes closed.

"What was so odd?" he asked. "He's a bright child. Your mother's face is new to him. It's not unusual for a baby to stare at strange people."

"Are you suggesting that my mother is strange?"

Patrick nudged Sophie's leg with a toe.

"You know what I mean. You bear a slight resemblance to your mother. He was probably just fascinated, that's all."

"She seemed to think it cut a little deeper than that."

"Meaning what? You think that little Max is developing a memory? Isn't he too young for that?"

"There are no iron-clad rules here. Where's the precedent? Maybe he was born with memories."

"Do you think he has memories of being Max or of being Bob?"

"I don't know. Either way, I think you're in for it."

"Hey, I can take him on with one hand tied behind my back."

"Don't take advantage of him. He's five feet shorter than you and he wears diapers."

The couple laughed quietly and reached for each other's hand. Connecting, they locked their fingers together.

"Do you think Idina will be spared memories?"

"I don't know. She just seems like a normal, happy little girl, so far. I would've expected my mother to have a stronger reaction to her, if you know what I mean."

"Idina was really out like a light tonight. I'll be curious to see how she behaves around your parents tomorrow."

Sophie started to chuckle.

"What's so funny?" asked Patrick.

"I can just picture tomorrow morning's scene. We throw the kids into bed with my mother and they both stare at her like *Children of the Corn*. I can already hear her screaming like Faye Wray in King Kong's fist."

"I sincerely hope that doesn't happen. I'll bet there are a lot of people in this complex with weak hearts."

Sophie breathed deeply. "I feel very peaceful right now," she said. "Let's have a great weekend. You'll meet some of my relatives. We'll go to the beach and build sandcastles with the kids. Maybe we'll see some exotic tropical animals on the golf course."

"Normal family stuff."

"If possible, yes, I'd love that."

"Sophie, how did your family handle your gift when you were a little girl? Did they encourage you? Discourage you?"

"After my adventure with Lila and those weird drawings, life became pretty ordinary. My parents looked at me like I was starring in *Rosemary's Baby* for a while, especially when I broke into Russian or predicted the future—boy, did that freak my mother out—but by the time I was five, my gift seemed to go into dormancy. I remained very close to my grandmother, but there was nothing unusual about our relationship. As she approached death, things got strange again."

"Strange? How?"

"I began to get glimpses of you. Oddly, you always looked the same. I never saw you as a child, only as a young adult—as I see you now. Will you ever change?"

"Of course. Now that we've reconnected in real time, you will see me age normally. We've caught up to one another."

"I think my mother is onto something. If she's looking at Max and seeing an old man's eyes, what do you think that means? Bobby wasn't an old man when he died."

"Neither was Max, Sophie. Keep in mind, Max was killed by accident when he was no older than I am now."

Sophie felt a sudden chill. She opened her eyes and looked sideways at Patrick's face, backlit and featureless in the dark. "Who can she be seeing, Patrick?"

"I sincerely don't know."

Sophie and Patrick both jumped when they heard a knock at the kitchen window behind them.

"It's getting late, kids," said Bill through the screen.

"Jesus, Dad, you scared us. We thought you went to bed."

"I did. I got up for a glass of water and heard voices. I thought maybe the TV was left on."

"Well, we told you we were going to sit in the Florida room. Did you happen to overhear what we were saying?"

Sophie flipped her legs over the side of the chaise and stared up at the window. All she saw was her father's shadow behind the screen. Her parents always loved to invade her privacy.

"No, of course not. I just got here. You really should get some sleep. We have a long day tomorrow."

"Really? What are we doing?"

"I don't know yet, but you're going to need your rest. Mother said something about company coming over for dessert."

"I'm exhausted already," said Sophie.

"Stay up as late as you like."

"No, we've talked enough. We'll see you tomorrow."

"Okay, then," said Bill, "I'm going back to bed. Good night."

"Night night," said Sophie and Patrick in unison. They sat in silence for a full two minutes before Sophie asked, "You think he heard anything?"

"What if he did? He probably wouldn't know what we were talking about anyway."

"I hope you're right."

As Bill walked back to the guest room, his only thought was, 'Did someone say something about a gift?' He wouldn't mention it to Roma. Let it be a surprise.

39

The family sat around the kitchen table, a sixty-inch circle of white Formica, surrounded by high-backed, blue-cushioned swivel chairs. The walls were covered in soft blue and green floral paper. A ceiling fan hung motionless overhead. Out the window, men and women in long plaid shorts and golf hats whacked balls and rode carts in the still-dewy grass. A second entry to the Florida room stood open behind Roma's chair, sending in the voices of the golfers as they passed within yards of the building.

Max and Idina sat in borrowed high chairs, eating Cheerios. Their bibs were dotted with mashed bananas and pureed peaches. Roma ran back and forth from the refrigerator in her housecoat and slippers with silver clips in her honey hair. The kitchen table was a chaotic still life of cereal boxes, assorted mismatched glasses and a dismembered newspaper, with coupons raggedly torn out. Sophie stood by the stove, expertly sectioning half grapefruits.

"Sit down already," said Bill, who sat combining Raisin Bran, Corn Chex and Cheerios in a white plastic bowl. Roma dashed over with a small pitcher of two-percent milk and poured it on his cereal.

"Who else needs anything?" she asked.

"Is there any yogurt or strawberries?" asked Sophie.

"No to the first; yes to the second. We picked them fresh from the farm."

"There's a farm on Jog Road?"

"It's more like a berry patch. Patrick, how about a couple of eggs?"

"No thanks, Roma. I'll make do with what's on the table. I love these *Everything* bagels."

"Why not? They've got everything."

Sophie put a half grapefruit in front of Patrick and one at her own place setting. Sitting down, her chair cushion emitted a hiss that made the babies laugh. Moments later, the wall clock starting cooing like a dove. Idina and Max laughed hysterically. Sophie stared at the clock and said, "What the hell was that?"

"That was the eight o'clock bird," said Roma. "Every hour of the day, between eight in the morning and eight in the evening, the clock makes different bird sounds. You're going to love the one o'clock bird. It makes a *schmock schmock* sound like Steve Allen. I almost bought *you* a bird clock."

Patrick started choking on his poppy seeds. Bill jumped up and pounded him on the back until Patrick put his arms up in surrender and declared himself saved. After drinking a full glass of water, Patrick said, "We would love a bird clock like that, wouldn't we kids?"

Idina and Max waved their arms and yelled, "Bird clock, bird clock."

"I don't know if they make them anymore," said Roma.

"Oh," said Patrick, reaching for the box of Raisin Bran. "Too bad."

Sophie asked, "What's on the agenda for today?"

Roma went to the window and said, "It's a beautiful day. I thought we'd go to the pool for a couple of hours. A lot of our friends would like to meet you and see the kids. We'd also like to show you the clubhouse. I have to be back here by five to start fixing dinner. Lenore and Dahlia are coming for dessert."

"Are Uncle Sy and Boris coming also?"

"Of course, they're coming. Everybody wants to see you."

"I guess I haven't seen them since Bob's and my wedding. They never made it for his funeral."

"What did you expect? He died in the winter. Floridians don't know how to deal with the cold."

"They're displaced New Yorkers, Ma. It's not like they were born and raised at the Miami Fountainbleu."

Sophie spooned a grapefruit wedge into her mouth and grimaced at its bitterness.

"Who wants some farmer cheese?" asked Bill.

"Biafra?" suggested Sophie.

Bill ignored her and asked, "Want to try it, Patrick?"

"Not today, Bill. I've had plenty. Thanks, though."

Idina and Max had enough of sitting at the table and started whining to be released from their high chairs. Patrick got up and lifted each of them over his head before lowering them gently to the ground. "Who wants to go swimming?" he asked the children.

"I don't think that babies in diapers are allowed in the big pool," said Bill.

Roma gave him a look and said, "That's why there's a kiddy pool."

"Also known as a cesspool," said Sophie. "Maybe we should all wear rubber suits."

"We don't have rubber suits," said Bill.

Roma started removing food and dishes from the table.

"Let's get dressed and get out of here. Before you know it, I'll have to run back here to fix the salad and bake the chicken. Who likes pasta with chicken?"

"Biafra?" suggested Sophie.

"I'll make sweet potatoes," said Roma.

Bill got up to rinse the plates and placed them on a drainer to dry. He said, "You all get ready to go. I've been dressed since five a.m. Don't forget to put sunscreen on the children. The sun can kill you here."

Roma said, "Hurry up, it's nearly nine. Let's make a day of it."

"And, I was so looking forward to the one o'clock bird," said Sophie.

40

Lenore and Sy, Dahlia and Boris arrived precisely on time, seven-sharp. A loon was warbling from the bird clock and the babies were laughing. Lenore and Sy brought an apple crumb cake and Dahlia and Boris brought cherry rugelach, all purchased at Publix. Roma had defrosted a Sara Lee pound cake, which she would serve with mocha almond fudge ice cream and Lipton tea. Everybody had declined coffee, except Patrick, who was addicted to it. Roma rummaged through her pantry and produced an antediluvian jar of instant Maxwell House. She set the pot to boil.

When Sophie heard the doorbell ring, she was still choking down the last of her chicken. She swallowed as quickly as possible and went running to open the door, along with Roma. Patrick stayed in the kitchen with the children and Bill hustled about clearing plates off the table.

"Sophie," Lenore and Dahlia screamed as they stepped into the foyer. The women held up their arms and Sophie fell into them, one at a time. She more sedately gave Sy and Boris feathery cheek kisses and light hugs. Sophie was happy to see how well they all looked, tanned and coifed and decked out in lime greens and pale pinks. The women were more subdued in black-and-white and taupe, but with huge, exotic rings, necklaces and earrings. Dahlia wore a jeweled parrot in her platinum hair.

"You should be a model with that figure," said Lenore, standing back and taking an appraising look at Sophie, standing tall in short shorts and a tank top. "Don't you think so, Dahlia? You'd never know she was the mother of twins."

"Sophie's always had a great body, but what about that gorgeous hunk your mother's been telling us about? And, how about those babies?"

As if on cue, Patrick walked in from the kitchen bearing Idina and Max in his sunburned arms. Bill also came in to greet the company and informed Roma that her water had boiled and he'd taken the kettle off the flame.

Sophie said, "Patrick, this is my Aunt Lenore and Uncle Sy, and my mother's cousin, Dahlia and her husband, Boris. Everybody, this is Patrick McKay." She bit her lip to keep from adding, *the father of my children.* "And, those little people in his arms are Idina and Max. Max is the one on the right."

Everybody clustered around Patrick and oohed and aahed over the babies. Dahlia lifted Idina's chin and said, "She sure looks like your Grandma Ida. You named her well. Look at that curly hair."

Idina gave Dahlia a smile before burying her head in Patrick's shoulder.

Max was staring intently at Lenore and Lenore was staring back. He held his arms out to her and Patrick allowed her to take him. The child clung tightly and clearly spoke her name, *Lenore.*

"Did you hear that?" Roma asked. She threw up her hands in exasperation "I've been trying to get him to call me Grandma all day but he just looks at me with those piercing blue eyes and says nothing. And, yet, here he goes calling you by name and he just met you." Roma put herself in front of Max and said, "Hey, what about Grandma?"

Max held out a hand and gently patted her face.

Everybody remarked on the gesture at once.

"That's a very unusual child," said Boris, who was an elementary school principal. "It's as if he's trying to comfort you."

"I just want him to call me Grandma," Roma moped.

"What about Idina?" Dahlia asked. "What does she call you?"

"Roma."

"Close enough."

"Who does Max look like?" puzzled Sy. "He has Sophie's hair like Idina does, but he doesn't look like his sister. Does he look like Bob? What do you think, Roma?"

"I think he looks like Patrick," said Lenore.

Everybody in the room froze and stared at Lenore—except Roma, who was giving Sophie the fisheye. Then she looked at Patrick and nodded to herself. She wouldn't fault Sophie's taste.

"What?" Lenore asked. "We were discussing looks. To me, he resembles Patrick—something in the expression—but I guess he has Bob's eyes. I don't remember Bob very well. The baby's just handsome, that's all."

Sophie and Patrick looked at each other and shrugged. They had kept their relationship under wraps until Bob had been gone a full year. For most of the world to know, Sophie and Patrick met when the children were already walking. Only Lt. Wiley, Officer Dwight and the Suffolk County coroner knew otherwise and their interest in Sophie and Patrick terminated before Sophie's pregnancy began to show. The autopsy that Wiley had finally insisted upon revealed that Bob was in perfect health and that he had no suspicious substances in his body before the trolley flattened him.

"There are lots of dark-haired, light-eyed guys running around. Let's just say that Max looks like himself," said Bill, sneaking a long look at Patrick.

"Let's all sit down and have dessert," Roma said.

Everybody shuffled into the kitchen and, amid a raucous scraping of chairs, settled around the table. The high chairs had been dispatched to the living room to make room for four more adult chairs and the babies were situated on Patrick and Sophie's laps. Desserts quickly appeared, along with plates, forks and cups. Roma threw a handful of sugar packets into the center of the table, as if she expected people to jump at them like birds at scattered breadcrumbs. Idina and Max immediately grabbed for anything within reach and everybody lurched forward to save them from themselves.

"Ma, can you please get me a couple of baby biscuits? There's a box of them on the counter."

Roma pulled out two cookies and rushed them over to her grandchildren. Dangling them over the babies' heads, she said, "Look, Grandma has doodoos."

Idina and Max looked perplexed.

"Ma, I don't want my children calling cookies doodoos. It's not dignified."

"That's what you used to call them."

"No, that's what *you* used to call them. To my children, doodoo means something entirely different, and it's probably not tasty."

Roma gave Sophie a look and pushed a biscuit into each sticky little hand.

"Here, kids, have a delicious *cookie*," she enunciated.

Idina and Max bit into their biscuits and squealed, "Doodoo" in unison.

"Thanks, Ma."

The company commented on how adorable and smart the children were.

"They're at that age where they repeat everything they hear," said Boris. "You have to watch what you say."

Bill raced around the table pouring water over teabags while Roma instructed the guests on which desserts to try and in which order. Bill said, "Keep the kids away from the cups. They can get scalded to death. Remember when you scalded Ron, Roma?"

"Roma gave him a look and said, "What are you talking about?"

Sophie and Patrick pushed back from the table and extended their hands all the way out to reach the rugelach. They kept their spare arms protectively wrapped around the kids' bellies, prepared to yank them out of harm's way. They were relieved the sun had set and golfers were no longer on the course aiming balls at the window behind their heads.

Halfway through dessert, Roma jumped up from the table and said, "I have a little surprise." She disappeared into the den and came back with a shoebox that was already old when Tom McCan was a boy or—as Bill would say—"When Hector was a pup."

"I have pictures," she sing-sang.

Sophie and Patrick looked at each other over their children's heads and had a collective thought: Here comes Pandora's box.

41

W e've seen those pictures a million times, already," said Lenore. She pressed a crumb off her plate with an index finger and popped it in her mouth.

"Patrick's never seen them," said Roma, already lifting the lid. "I'll bet there are some in here that Sophie's never seen."

Roma picked out her high school graduation picture and passed it to Sophie saying, "Your mama wasn't too bad looking."

Actually, Roma was drop-dead gorgeous at eighteen. Sophie shared the black-and-white photograph with Patrick and he said, "What a beautiful picture." He passed the photo to Lenore who nodded and passed it on to Sy, who was licking ice cream off his spoon.

"I take after my father," said Roma. "That's where I get the blue eyes." She batted her short straight lashes at Patrick.

"It's a great shot, Ma."

Roma pulled out pictures of she and Bill at nightclubs and weddings, kissing in a rowboat, smiling expansively at their newborns. There were pictures of cousins, still living but mostly forgotten. They'd been left behind in New York. There were small tan folders containing series of photos, of Ron and Sophie playing in a wheelbarrow, swinging bats, posing in life jackets beside some long-forgotten bungalow colony pool. The company perked up when they recognized their own young selves and their own children.

"Look at us," they all said.

"I remember Nana Sofia's house like it was yesterday," said Dahlia, raising her glasses to take a closer look at the picture before her. Nana Sofia was sitting on a chair in the front parlor, her gray hair up in braids. Gershon stood behind her, grave-faced, a hand on her shoulder.

Ida sat beside her mother. Two blond children sat at their feet, Roma and her little sister, Lenore.

"I guess my father must've taken that picture," remarked Roma. "Otherwise, he'd be in the picture."

"Your great-grandmother was a very special woman, Sophie," said Dahlia. "I was very close to her as a child."

"What was she like?"

"She was not educated, but she was very intelligent and resourceful. She managed a large household on a shoestring and I never heard a complaint out of her. Her family was her whole life. She was tough and earthy—she hadn't had an easy time of it—but she knew how to love. I miss her to this day."

"What about Zayde?"

"I think he gave your grandmother plenty of trouble early on, but they were very devoted to each other. Nana told me he had a bit of the wild seed in him, but something happened that settled him down completely. Don't ask me what—Nana would never tell me. I'll tell you one thing: He was crazy about you. You have no idea how upset he was when we thought we might lose you."

"Really? I wish I had a better memory of him."

Roma rifled through the pictures and stopped abruptly. With a tongue in her cheek, she handed Sophie a small photo and said, "Here's one I don't think you've ever seen."

Bill looked at Roma's face and asked, "Why the melodrama?"

Roma ignored him and watched her daughter.

Sophie reeled as she took in the contents of the photo and nearly dropped Max off her lap. An elderly man with long white hair stood looking at an infant in his arms. The tender, unspoken exchange between man and child was so focused, so potent, that Sophie was stricken with the memory of looking into her great-grandfather's eyes and knowing him completely; knowing his secrets, knowing his love and knowing that his beloved Sofia had been returned to him. They were Gershon's eyes. They were Patrick's eyes. Sophie felt hot tears coursing down her cheeks.

Patrick leaned forward and kissed her cheek. Sophie kept her eyes closed and wept. The table fell silent, until the bird clock hooted like an owl. It was the final birdcall of the day—the eight p.m. bird. Idina and Max were too engrossed watching their mother cry to laugh.

When she was able to speak, Sophie asked, "Where and when did you find this?"

"Here and now."

"I don't understand. Haven't you been looking at these photos for years?"

"I haven't looked at them since your grandmother died. When we cleaned out her apartment, we took her photos and mixed them in with ours. I guess this one escaped our notice."

"Who took the picture?"

"Probably your Grandpa Gabe. He was the picture taker in the family."

"Had you ever seen this picture before?"

"I don't recall ever seeing it. It had to be taken just before he died. In fact, it may be the last picture ever taken of him."

Sophie dried her eyes with the back of her hand and said, "Do you think there are any more of him and me?"

"I don't know. Let's divvy up the pile and check, since we're all here anyway. Let's clean off the table first so nothing gets wet. What do you say?"

Everybody was in agreement, so, after the table had been cleared and wiped dry, Roma distributed clumps of photos and said, "This should bring back some memories."

As Patrick watched Sophie's family go through the old photos, he knew they would find no other pictures of Sophie and her great-grandfather. The picture of Sophie and Gershon had come from his parents' attic. He had carried the picture in his billfold since the night he and Sophie had met, waiting for the right occasion to share it with her. He felt it would be best if she saw it in the presence of her family. While everyone had chatted and distracted themselves with sweets, he had slipped the picture out of his billfold and placed it in the box. He knew that Sophie would insist upon keeping it.

Amid much commentary and laughter, the family pored through the photos, separating some out for further scrutiny or identification. New piles began to take shape. Max finally nodded off, his head drooping down on his chest.

With no birds going off, Sophie had lost track of the time. It was nearly ten when she looked at the clock and said, "My God, it's late. We've got to get these kiddies to bed. Would you all excuse us?"

As Sophie and Patrick rose to a chorus of "Of courses," Bill asked, "What has Idina got there?"

Wide-eyed in her father's arms, Idina held a picture tightly in her fist. When Roma tried to take the picture from her, the baby tugged it back and started to scream.

"Goodness, this is the first time I've heard her carry on since she got here," said Bill, patting the child and trying to calm her down. "Show Grandpa the picture, Idina. Let's see what's got you all upset."

Idina shook her head violently and continued to wail. Max, miraculously, remained asleep.

"Let her keep it for now," said Sophie. "I don't want it to get torn and she's got quite a grip on her—stronger than Max's. I'll give it back to you after she falls asleep."

"It's getting late, sweetheart," said Lenore. "We're going to have to leave pretty soon ourselves. Maybe we should say our good-byes now. We'll see you again before you leave."

"Okay, Aunt Lenore. It actually may take a while to settle Idina down. She seems pretty worked up. She's usually very placid. I think she's just plain over-tired."

Sophie made the rounds and kissed the cheeks of everyone at the table. "Thanks for coming and visiting with us and helping us sort through all these pictures. We sure put you all to work."

"It was a pleasure, darling," said Dahlia. "So many memories and such a wonderful surprise, that picture of you with Zayde. It was so nice to meet you, Patrick. We hope we see a whole lot more of you."

"I'm sure you will, Dahlia. It's good to finally meet some of Sophie's family. I'll look forward to the next time."

Shortly thereafter, Sophie and Patrick heard voices in the living room and then a door open and shut. They were able to calm Idina down with a bottle and a backrub, but the baby still held on to the picture she had pilfered from the table. When she finally drifted off, Patrick picked her up and placed her next to her brother and tucked her in, gently extricating the picture from her sweaty hand.

Examining the photo under a lamp, Sophie got her second jolt of the evening.

"What is it?" asked Patrick.

"It's a fairly recent picture of my grandmother with Lila and Jeanette. Now, why would that make my baby girl cry?"

New York 1953

42

Ida and Gabe had turned a corner of their bedroom into a nursery. There was space for a cradle beside the room's only window. The window faced a back alley, strewn with clotheslines and debris but it was the brightest spot in the dim room. Ida felt strongly that babies needed light to grow, like flowers.

Beside the cradle was a brocade rocker, a relic that Gershon's uncle had carried over from Latvia, probably on his back. The chair had previously been in Sofia and Gershon's apartment and all of the Polokov children had been rocked in it. It was the only piece of furniture that Gershon kept when Sofia died. When he moved in with his daughter and son-in-law, the chair came with him.

Today, he sat in the rocker and gazed at his great-granddaughter's face. The rest of the family was in the living room, watching *Truth or Consequences*. Soon, they would finish dessert and go, and they would take newborn Sophie with them. He pressed a fist into his chest. There was so much to say and so little time. He didn't fret over what the baby might understand or not understand. He would share with her what was in his heart.

"Dear one," he began, "I am so happy you have returned to me, if even for a moment. Soon, you will be carried off into your new life and I will be carried off into mine. It doesn't matter where we go or how we go. I will never be far from you. You are all I've ever lived for."

Gershon reached over the cradle and gently caressed Sophie's petal-soft hand with the dry pad of his thumb. Her long fingers constricted into a fist and Gershon smiled. "Still a little fighter, I see. Good."

Gershon eased back into the chair and said, "So, my little Sophie, I will tell you all that you need to know in the short time that's left to us.

"Above all, you should know that your great-grandmother and I were very much in love. It's not that we didn't have our troubles. Sofia lost our only son when I was far away from her and of no use. But, I want to tell you that someday, when you're grown, you will marry a young man, and together you will give birth to this lost boy. How do I know this? I know because I, too, was a son reborn. With advancing age, my memory for past lives has faded, but visions of the future have grown sharper. I will live again and, in the next life, I will make amends.

"In this life, I was born to a family that was foreign to me. That is why I needed to leave. My son was born to the right family, but he was born too soon. He's been waiting for you. When he comes, he will surprise everybody but most of all, his father. This child will be born to render love. He will be endowed with intelligence, sensitivity and vivid recall."

A gentle knock came at the door. Ida peeked into the room and asked, "Dad, is the baby all right?"

"Why shouldn't she be all right? She's with her Zayde. We're having a nice visit."

"Bill and Roma would like to get going pretty soon."

"What's the rush?"

"Roma's tired."

"Please, a little more time," begged Gershon.

Ida said, "Okay, Dad," and backed out.

When the door was closed, Gershon said, "Where was I? Oh, yes. I was telling you that you would bear an unexpected son. You will also bear a daughter and she will come as no surprise, but she won't be who you think she is. Am I confusing you, Sophie? I'm sorry, sweetheart. But, I'm getting ahead of myself. Indulge me a little longer and I will finish my story.

"After I escaped from the army and settled in America, I was able to bring your great-grandmother and her dear friend, Lila, to this country. This time, Sofia brought me a strong, healthy child conceived before I left Russia—your Grandma Ida.

After a while, I introduced Lila to a very good man, named Max Birnbaum. Lila's still alive and you will love her. You will also be happy to know that Lila will reappear in your future, but don't expect her to know you. She will not have memories.

"Max was a much better man than I was, and he also loved your great-grandmother. When Sofia first came to this country, I made some effort to be a good man. I was always hardworking. Unfortunately, the bad habits of my youth returned and this grieved Sofia. My family was starving and, in my drunken stupidity, I thought that Sofia would be better off without me. I was a coward. Max died trying to keep me from killing myself. It was an accident, but the horror of it never left me. Sofia and I got on with our lives, sharing this terrible burden.

The baby started to whimper and Gershon calmed her with a caress.

"Here's what you need to know about Max, dear Sophie. Someday, you will meet a man. He will seem very familiar to you and you will marry him. He will be Max reborn. He will finally get to be with the woman he loves. That will be his reward, but your marriage will not last and you will not bear his children. You will only be able to bear children with one man, and that man will be your one true husband. Someday, you and this man will give rebirth to Max and he will finally be where he safely belongs. His memory will be strong, but he will be evolved enough to render forgiveness instead of revenge."

Another knock came at the door. This time it was Gabe.

"Pop," he said, "it's getting late."

Gershon held a finger to his lips and said, "Shhhh, I think she's almost asleep."

"It's time for the baby to go home with her parents and brother, Pop. You'll see her again soon, I promise."

"Please," said Gershon, "one more minute. We are almost finished here."

Gabe looked at his father-in-law and asked, "Is everything okay, Pop?"

"Sure, sure. What shouldn't be okay? Sophie and I are getting to know each other. We're having the most wonderful visit. Please, tell everybody, we're almost through."

Gabe said, "One more minute, Pop," and left the room.

When the door was closed, Gershon got up and placed his face near the baby's and looked into her eyes. He stroked her cheek with a finger and said, "Little one, I have one more thing to tell you before we part."

The infant listened without moving her eyes from her great-grandfather's face.

"I didn't believe that Sofia was meant to be reborn. I thought we were both finished with this cycle of rebirth. When you were born a year to the day after Sofia died, I tried to convince myself that you weren't Sofia reborn. Then I saw you, and there was no question that you were she. That's when I knew I wasn't finished here. For the first time, I focused on a future I never expected to have. I saw a new life unfold for us and, when it's over, we will finally be allowed to leave for good.

"When you survived your difficult birth, the first person you saw was your Grandma Ida. You are the infant now and she is your grandmother, but she was once your daughter and she will become your daughter again. You will be the last person your grandmother sees in this life. Before she dies, she will tell you to watch for me. It is only through our union that she will be reborn, and she is being born to carry us forward. She alone will render onto us eternal release. That is the gift that she brings."

Gershon gazed out the window and sighed. Long shadows were forming in the back alley and women were calling their children to dinner. Gershon looked into Sophie's guileless eyes and smiled.

"Time to go now, my love," He said. "Don't worry about all that I've told you. You've got a life to live and maybe I'm just a crazy old man, full of fairy stories. Forget everything I've told you, except this: I will always find you."

Gershon lifted the baby from her cradle and held her aloft. At that moment, Gabe entered the room with his camera and said, "Hold that pose."

In the explosive white light of the flash, Sophie saw the face of a young man with long black hair and clear, pale eyes.

That night, Gershon Polokov died peacefully in his sleep.

READER'S GUIDE

1. Did Sophie craft a life based on her dying great-grandfather's prophecies or was she truly at the end of a long series of lives? Where does suggestion end and memory begin?

2. When Gershon (now Patrick) first presents himself to Sophie, she is three years old and he's a full-grown man. Why do you think Patrick's character is always the same age until he and Sophie connect as adults?

3. How do you suppose Gershon/Patrick can find Sophie wherever she is? Can he appear and disappear at will or does he only exist as a projection of Sophie's memory until they truly connect when they are both adults?

4. Sophie's grandmother, Ida, suspects that her granddaughter has special gifts. How do Ida's memories play into the story? Why does she keep Sophie's secret to herself?

5. Why does Sophie seem estranged from her own parents and brother?

6. What is the significance of Sophie's relationship with Lila/Mrs. Stern (Bob's mother)?

7. Do Sophie's pictures of the young Gershon and the young Lila have a life of their own?

8. Mrs. Stern gives Sophie a sapphire and diamond necklace and matching earrings. Sophie's mother, Roma, gives her a sapphire and diamond ring. Is Roma capable of recognizing that the jewelry is part of the same set and what the significance of that is?

9. Are relationships and actions believable in each lifetime? For example, does it make sense that certain actions are repeated (Max/Bob's accidental death at the hands of Gershon/Patrick)? Are people destined to repeat the same actions lifetime after lifetime until they all reach a point of mutual memory?

10. Why do you suppose there are time warps in the story? For example, when Bob goes into the basement to search for Lila and Gershon's pictures, several hours out of his life disappear. How can this be explained?

11. Does Sophie want to be with Patrick or is she only destined to be with him? Does choice play a role here?

12. Sophie and Patrick's daughter, Idina, is presented as the one who will relieve them of the cycle of birth and rebirth. Have Sophie and Patrick learned what they're supposed to learn from life on an earthly plane so they can move forward?

13. It appears that Sophie and Patrick's son, Max, has been born with memories of being an earlier iteration of Max and Bob, Sophie's former husband whom Patrick accidentally scares to death. Does Patrick have something to fear from his son in the future?

14. If you believe that you have lived multiple lifetimes with the same cast of characters, have you personally connected with anyone from past lives? If so, do they share your memories?

15. Would you choose to come back to life on this plane—and, if so, for what purpose?

www.ingramcontent.com/pod-product-compliance
Lightning Source LLC
Chambersburg PA
CBHW031948010726
47493CB00007B/2129